LONG TERM CARE MONITORING FOR QUALITY RESIDENT MEAL TIME FOOD AND NUTRITION
SERVICES REVISED

This book must be used in addition to the current CMS Federal Long Term Care Regulations as CMS periodically issues revisions to the Federal F-Tags and Interpretive Guidelines. This book is not a substitute for the published Long Term Care Regulations.

While the author has used her best efforts in preparing this book, she makes no representations or warranties with respect to the completeness of the contents of this book.

LONG TERM CARE MONITORING FOR QUALITY RESIDENT MEAL TIME FOOD AND NUTRITION SERVICES REVISED

by

Nora Wellington

ReadersMagnet, LLC

Long Term Care Monitoring for Quality Resident Meal Time Food and Nutrition Services Revised
Copyright © 2019 by Nora Wellington. All rights reserved.

Published in the United States of America
ISBN Paperback: 978-1-950947-52-2
ISBN eBook: 978-1-950947-53-9

Available on www.norawellingtonbooks.com and www.amazon.com

All rights reserved. No part of this publication may be reproduced, stored in a retrieval system or transmitted in any way by any means, electronic, mechanical, photocopy, recording or otherwise without the prior permission of the author except as provided by USA copyright law.

The opinions expressed by the author are not necessarily those of ReadersMagnet, LLC.

ReadersMagnet, LLC
10620 Treena Street, Suite 230 | San Diego, California, 92131 USA
1.619.354.2643 | www.readersmagnet.com

Book design copyright © 2019 by ReadersMagnet, LLC. All rights reserved.

Cover design by Ericka Walker
Interior design by Shemaryl Evans

CONTENTS

Foreword 7

Acknowledgments 11

About The Author 13

Introduction 15

Part I

State Operations Manual (Chapter 7) 21

Terminologies & Definitions 23

Additional Definitions 27

Survey Process 32

When Surveyors Walk Through Your Doors 35

Entrance Conference Worksheet 37

Part II

New F-Tags 47

How To Use The Monitoring Tools 48

Regulations & F-Tags For Resident Meal Time And Dining Experience 50

Resident Meal Time And Dining Experience Monitoring Tool 74

Regulation F-Tags For Kitchen And Food Service 86

F-Tags For Kitchen And Food Service 87

Kitchen And Food Service Monitoring Tool 97

Part III

Enforcement Process–Brief Synopsis 105

Acceptable Plan Of Correction 106

Revisits And Verifying Facility Compliance 108

Enforcement Process 110

The Deficiency Matrix 112

References 113

FOREWORD

It is usually stated that there are over of 15,500 nursing homes in the United States that are certified either Medicaid or Medicare or both. There are also about 1.3 million people, including elderly and disabled people who receive care each day in nursing homes. Nursing homes certified as Medicare are called Skilled Nursing Facilities (SNFs), and nursing homes certified as Medicaid are called Nursing Facilities (NFs). A lot of the nursing homes are certified as both Medicare and Medicaid and these are referred to as dual certified. A 2015 assessment or study was completed that is titled "Reading the Stars: Nursing Home Quality Star Ratings, Nationally and by State" revealed some findings about the data analysis in the Centers for Medicare & Medicaid Services (CMS) Five-Star Quality Rating System, in the Nursing Home Compare website for consumers. Nursing Home Compare is usually utilized by consumers who are looking to place their families and their loved ones in a nursing home or a SNF or a NF, but it is also recommended by CMS that the nursing home compare star system should be used as one of the tools not the only tool in families' decision making process. These are a few of the key findings:

- More than one-third of nursing homes certified by Medicare or Medicaid have relatively low overall star of 1 or 2 stars, accounting for 30 percent of all nursing home residents. Conversely, 45 percent of the nursing homes have overall ratings of 4 or 5 stars, accounting for 41 percent of all nursing homes residents.

- In 11 states, at least 40 percent of nursing homes in the state have relatively low ratings (1 or 2 stars). In 22 states and the District of Columbia, at least 50 percent of the nursing homes in the state have relatively high overall ratings (4 or 5 stars)[1]

Those of us in the long term care community are aware that the Federal regulations are now revised and the Centers for Medicare & Medicaid did establish three Phases for implementation for the revised regulations. All revised regulations that affected Phase 1 became effective November 28, 2016, those affecting Phase 2 became effective November 28, 2017, and those revised regulations affecting Phase 3 will become effective November 28, 2019. The F-Tags are also newly numbered

---

1 Reading the Stars: Nursing Home Quality Star Ratings, Nationally and State, Kaiser Foundation, May 2015, Cristina Boccuti, Giselle Casillas, Tricia Neuman, page 1.

F-tags. CMS provided a crosswalk from the old F-tags to the new F-tags. So Administrators and Directors of Nursing, if you need to reference the new F-tags, and need a copy of the F-tag crosswalk, you can access the CMS.gov website. The web address is https://cms.gov/medicare/provider-enrollment-and-certification/guidanceforlawsand regulations/nursing-homes.html

For those that may not be aware, during the process of revising the regulations in 2016, CMS put out a request for comments to the final rule, to get comments from the public as part of the process. CMS received a total of 9,800 public comments from the following groups–from long term care consumers, from advocacy groups, from ombudsman's groups, from organizations representing providers of long term care, from state survey agencies, from legal organizations, and from many individual health care professionals. All the comments and CMS' responses to those comments were published in Vol.81, October 4, 2016 Federal Register. As a hands-on administrator of twenty-seven plus years, who also is very passionate about patient care, about quality and regulatory compliance, I spent some time reading through these comments and responses. Below is one of those comments and CMS' corresponding response to that comment that was tugging at me while I was reading through this section of the Federal Register.

Comments:

"Some commenters also expressed concern that CMS may be unreasonably focused on regulating LTC facilities, to the point of not updating regulations and requirements for other provider types. Commenters also claimed that LTC facilities are "the most regulated industry in America." And that "the nuclear industry is less regulated" than the LTC facility industry."

CMS Response:

"We recognize that the proposed rule and this final rule are large, detailed documents, and that many individuals relied on summaries to learn about the proposed requirements. We understand that working professionals and family caregivers can be very busy, but we are concerned about some of these misinterpretations. Most of the misconceptions fell into three categories: Unfamiliarity with the old requirements, misunderstanding of the proposed requirements, or confusion about which facilities must meet the LTC requirements. The comments displaying unfamiliarity with the existing requirements are troubling to us."[2]

This book, Long Term Care Monitoring for Quality Resident Meal Time Food and Nutrition Services Revised, **is designed for easy-to-read and easy-to-follow format, and a quick reference guide** for the long term care community. It will benefit administrators, directors of nursing, QAPI

---

[2] From the Federal Register / Vol. 81, No. 192/ Tuesday October 4, 2016/ Rules and Regulations page 8.

directors, staff development directors/coordinators, food service directors/managers, and dietitians to help them help their residents.

The book will help staffs:

- Become a lot more familiar with the revised regulations and new F-tags on Food & Nutrition Services as it is designed in an easy-to-read and easy-to-follow format.

- Become more familiar with the new survey process, and State Operations Manual.

- Monitor more routinely for compliance with regulations as expected by CMS

- Monitor more routinely for Quality of Care and Quality of Life for the residents they serve in their facilities.

ACKNOWLEDGMENTS

THIS IS TO SAY SPECIAL THANKS TO my friends, colleagues, and other long term care professionals and facility administrators who purchased my first two books, "The Fundamentals of Quality for Long Term Care Part 1" and "Long Term Care Monitoring Tools Resident Meal Time and Dining Experience Kitchen & Food Service."

I also want to say thanks to a dear friend, who shall remain nameless for now; she knows who she is. Thank you for our chats, for helping keep me motivated, and for your input.

Finally, to my family: Dudley Sr., Dudley II, Melissa, Neal, Casey, and Cole; and to all my siblings and my nephews and nieces for your continued support and for our family love that continues to grow. With continued thanks.

ABOUT THE AUTHOR

Nora Wellington, MBA, LNHA, Certified Interact Champion, is the CEO / Founder of N Wellington Associates LLC (www.nwellingtonassociates.com), and author of two books, Long Term Care Monitoring Tools Resident Meal Time Dining Experience Kitchen and Food Service, published 2012. The Fundamentals of Quality for Long Term Care, Part 1, co-author with Alicia Creighton-Allen, published 2010. Wellington has twenty-seven plus years of long term care (LTC) hands-on administrator experience, and over thirty years in the long term care industry. She served in her permanent position as administrator in three skilled nursing facilities during a seventeen-year period in her career, before she became an entrepreneur and a consultant helping facilities with their overall operations, with leadership, survey preparation, and regulatory compliance & QAPI. Her consulting services also includes interim administrator, development of effective Plan of Correction with timely implementation. She directs skilled nursing facilities (SNFs) and nursing facilities (NF) to the path of quality and regulatory compliance. N Wellington Associates also provide educational in-services, and leadership development.

Early in Wellington's nursing home administrator career, she was fortunate to have been hired in 1996 to help a hospital open a brand new hospital-based skilled nursing facility when the hospital made a decision to expand its continuum of care for the community. Through Wellington's hard work with the director of nursing, and the hospital's project director they were successful in accomplishing all aspects of the requirements, including the physical environment, life safety code, and the development of all administrative and clinical policies and procedures. The initial certification survey was successful and Wellington became the leader and nursing home administrator of this brand new Medicare & Medicaid certified hospital-based SNF where she provided leadership for eleven plus years. Within a year of the hospital-based facility opened, Wellington also successfully secured a Joint Commission accreditation for the facility. As the nursing home administrator in this acute care hospital setting, Wellington developed educational in-services on long term care regulations, on survey protocol and on the importance of regulatory compliance for resident physicians, for acute care nurses, for certified nursing assistants and for other disciplines. Through the years she developed a passion for patient care, for quality and for the long term care profession.

Wellington is a hands-on administrator. She is hard working consultant; she is caring and dedicated and committed to her work, and she believes in growth and self-development. Whenever her assignment includes interim administrator, she will devote about thirty percent of her work day being with her clinical management staff, conducting rounds on the unit sometimes independently and other times with environment of care rounds teams, spending time with residents. She loves spending time on the unit because this gives her the opportunity to observe, monitor and interact with both staff and residents. Also this gives her opportunity to observe first-hand operational issues. Through the years, she has designed several monitoring tools for use internally in the facilities that she has served as administrator. As an administrator, Wellington enjoys making a positive impact and she uses any and all opportunities to help staffs at all levels.

Wellington always receives positive feedback from owners and/or corporate leaders for her consulting work at the SNFs and NFs for efficiency of the operations and successful survey preparation and outcomes. Her clients include facilities of national, regional, and local long term care organizations. She takes pride in her work.

She has also designed training workshops and did presentations on topics such as "Effective Communication Skills with Focus on Assertiveness", "Customer Service Effectiveness", and "Team Building" for small size organizations.

Wellington graduated with MBA from George Washington University, in Washington, DC. She also attended the University of Maryland University College (UMUC) to do her course work in Gerontology, Ageing & Disability, and Long Term Care Administration. Because of her desire to continue to teach as well as to be a lifelong learner, Wellington also became a Certified INTERACT Champion.

INTRODUCTION

IN JUNE 2019 TWO PENNSYLVANIA U.S. SENATORS published a report titled "Families' and Residents' Right to Know: Uncovering Poor Care in America's Nursing Homes." This report acknowledges that many older Americans benefit from the care that is provided by nursing home staff, but the report also focuses on the poor performing facilities particularly those facilities that are classified as poor performing Special Focus Facilities (SFF). In May 2019, the Senators requested the list from the Centers for Medicare & Medicaid Services, and as of June 4, 2019, the listing of all facilities that are participants in the SFF program and those that are candidates as of April 2019, were provided to the Senators by the Centers for Medicare & Medicaid Services, and that list was released to the public, because the Senators believe that the list should be publicly available to individuals and families who may need to make a decision on which nursing home to select for their loved ones. Both Pennsylvania Senators believe that this list of SFF should be public knowledge, as it will help consumers in their decision making process.

Of the more than 15,700 nursing homes nationwide, less than 0.6% (a maximum of 88 facilities) is selected for the program (SFF program). The names of these facilities are made public.[3] An additional 2.5% of facilities (approximately 400 facilities) qualify for the program because they are identified as having persistent record of poor care" but are not selected for participation as a result of limited resources at the Centers for Medicare & Medicaid Services (CMS).[4] It must be noted here that this list was once known to CMS and the facilities that were SFF, and was not made public.

Administrators and directors of nursing mainly must be aware that the Centers for Medicare and Medicaid Services (CMS) have established and outlined their expectations for skilled nursing facilities (SNFs) and for nursing facilities (NFs) during the process of revising the federal regulations. The State Surveyors on behalf of CMS reinforces those CMS expectations when

---

[3] Families' And Residents' Right to Know: Uncovering Poor Care in America's Nursing Homes: Report by U.S. Senator Bob Casey (D-PA and U.S. Senator Pat Toomey (R-PA), U.S. Senate Website newsroom release.

[4] Families And Residents' Right to Know: Uncovering Poor Care In America's Nursing Homes: Report by U.S. Senator Bob Casey (D-PD) and U.S. Senator Pat Toomey (R-PA), U.S. Senate Website newsroom release.

they walk into your facilities for annual surveys or complaint surveys. A focus now continues to be placed on facilities to monitor their performance for quality in their buildings. So on a daily routine basis, administrators and their teams should have their expectations for patient care, for quality, for the environment, and for regulatory compliance. Here are few questions that staff must always ask themselves and answer on a daily routine basis.

- Does the facility look neat and clean with no odor?

- Do the residents looked well groomed, or are they wearing clothes with food stain or food particles on them?

- Are staffs interacting well with residents, or are residents sitting in their wheelchairs lined up in the hallway at the nurses' station?

- And for the kitchen, does the food service staff keep and maintain a clean sanitary environment with clean floors in the kitchen?

- Are the food service staffs following food safety protocol?

As stated above, the nursing home reform regulation implemented by CMS starting with Phase 1 in November 2016, established several expectations to help facilities remain in substantial compliance with the requirements of participation in the Medicare & Medicaid program. One cannot overemphasize the importance of facilities staying in substantial compliance with the new requirements of participation. Survey is now more stringent and remedies are applied appropriately for non-compliance with the requirements of participation. Listed below are three important expectations:

1. **Expectation #1:** It is expected that all Skilled Nursing Facilities (SNFs) and Nursing Facilities (NFs) or nursing homes as is sometimes called generically (providers), routinely stay in substantial compliance with the Federal Long Term Care the State law and Long Term Care Regulations.

2. **Expectation # 2:** CMS expects that Skilled Nursing Facilities and Nursing Facilities who have deficiencies during their surveys must address all deficiencies promptly.

3. **Expectation # 3:** CMS expects that residents admitted to these facilities the SNFs and NFs will receive the care and services they need to meet their highest practicable level of functioning.

For Food and Nutrition Services (§ 483.60):

- The revised reform regulation is requiring facilities to provide each resident with a nourishing, palatable, well-balanced diet that meets his or her daily nutritional and special dietary needs, taking into consideration the preferences of each resident. CMS is also requiring facilities to employ sufficient staff, including the designation of a director of food and nutrition service, with the appropriate competencies and skill sets to carry out the functions of dietary services while taking into consideration resident assessments and individual plans of care, including diagnoses and acuity, as well as the facility's resident census.

- For administrators, directors of nursing, and also the Food Service Directors or Managers, the new survey process directs surveyor(s) to the kitchen as one of the first location as soon as they arrive at the facility. So the kitchen must be survey ready 365 days a year.

This book gives the administrator, the director of nursing and your staffs an accessible reference guide that is *easy-to-read and easy-to-follow* offering monitoring tools that focus on select topic areas in dining experience for residents and for the food service department, for designated disciplines and/or departments to assist staffs increase their knowledgebase, become more familiar with these regulations. CMS has established ongoing routine monitoring as one of the major expectations for SNFs and NFs. We can acknowledge that facility administrators and their QAPI programs establish plans for routine monitoring, however those plans get held back sometimes by unexpected realities such as staff call-outs, or incidences of emergency situations that have to be attended to. But routine monitoring none the less, should not be put on hold. Monitoring helps staffs provide Quality of care for residents.

This book is divided into three parts as outlined below.

- **Part I** contains synopsis of the State Operations Manual (SOM) including important Definitions, Survey Protocol and Process, that the Administrator, Director of Nursing, Department Heads and staff should be knowledgeable about.

- **Part II** contains compilation of the new and reform Federal Long Term Care Regulations that relate to Resident Meal Time & Dining Experience Kitchen and Food Service and the Monitoring Tools for those areas. The regulations are compiled in an easy-to-read and easy-to-follow format.

- **Part III** contains brief Synopsis of the Enforcement Protocol with a listing of Remedies for non-compliance of the Federal Regulations.

<u>Long Term Care Monitoring for Quality Resident Meal Time Food and Nutrition Services Revised</u> is based on the current Federal Long Term Care Regulations as of November 28, 2017 and the Survey and Enforcement Protocol as of November 16, 2018. It incorporates the Federal Regulations of Phase I and Phase II. As all in the long term care community and the long term care industry know, the regulations are very detailed and voluminous. Skilled Nursing Facilities and Nursing Facilities have a total of I believe 205 Federal F-Tags, and of course the states have their State Regulations, also all disciplines have their protocol and practice manuals, and the Life Safety Code Regulations. For all surveys that are happening currently, the expectation is that facilities must be in substantial compliance with the regulations and with the requirements of participation. Phases I and II of the revised reform regulations have already been implemented as stated, and Phase III have an implementation date of November 28, 2019.

STATE OPERATIONS MANUAL (SOM)

BRIEF SYNOPSIS

DEFINITIONS

&

SURVEY PROCESS

STATE OPERATIONS MANUAL (CHAPTER 7)

SYNOPSIS OF PORTIONS OF THE STATE OPERATIONS MANUAL

SURVEY AND ENFORCEMENT PROCESS FOR SKILLED NURSING FACILITIES AND NURSING FACILITIES

REVISION DATE OF NOVEMBER 16, 2018

CHAPTER 7 OF THE STATE OPERATIONS MANUAL (SOM) covers the implementation of the new nursing home survey, certification, and enforcement regulations at 42 CFR Part 488. It is important that administrators and staffs take seriously the fact that the Centers for Medicare & Medicaid Services (CMS) continues to stress the need for facilities to maintain substantial compliance with the reform regulations and with the requirements of participation with the Medicare & Medicaid programs. Below are the expectations established through the reform regulations for nursing homes, skilled nursing facilities (SNFs) and nursing facilities (NFs) are listed below. Note that the words skilled nursing facilities (SNFs), nursing facilities (NFs) and nursing homes are used interchangeably throughout the book.

Expectations that CMS has mandated through the reform nursing home regulations for SNFs and NFs:

- **The first expectation** by CMS is that providers (SNFs/NFs/nursing homes) remain in substantial compliance with Medicare & Medicaid program requirements as well as with State law.

    - CMS expects that SNFs/NFs maintain continued rather than cyclical compliance.

- CMS also mandates through the enforcement process that SNFs/NFs establish policies and procedures to address deficiencies and deficient practices to ensure that correction is lasting.

- CMS also expects that facilities take the initiative and responsibility for continuously monitoring their own performance to sustain compliance.

- CMS also expects measures such as the requirements for an acceptable plan of correction emphasize that facilities should have the ability to achieve and maintain compliance leading to improved quality of care.

- **The second expectation** by CMS is that all deficiencies which resulted out of a survey must be addressed promptly.

    - The standard for program participation mandated by the regulation is substantial compliance.

    - The State and CMS Regional Office will take steps to bring about compliance quickly after the survey findings.

    - Below are some of the enforcement remedies that can be imposed before a facility has the opportunity to correct its deficiencies:

        - Civil monetary penalties.

        - Temporary managers.

        - Directed Plan of Correction.

        - In-Service Training.

        - Denial of Payment for New Admissions.

        - State Monitoring may on occasion be imposed before the SNF/NF have the opportunity to correct its deficiencies.

- **The third expectation** by CMS through the reform regulations is that residents will receive the care and services they need to meet their highest practicable level of functioning.

This point cannot be overemphasized, that SNFs, NFs and nursing homes must be in substantial compliance of these regulations in order to continue participation in the Medicare & Medicaid programs.

TERMINOLOGIES & DEFINITIONS

BELOW ARE TERMINOLOGIES AND ACRONYMS, WITH DEFINITIONS as defined by CMS. These are important terminologies to help administrators, directors of nursing, department heads and staffs increase their knowledgebase and comfort level with the work they do.

- **Abbreviated Standard Survey**–is a short survey when information is gathered through resident-centered techniques to determine compliance with participation. This type of survey could originate from complaint by residents or families, a change in ownership, a change in administrator or director of nursing, or other concerns.

- **Abuse** means the willful infliction of injury, unreasonable confinement, intimidation, or punishment with resulting of physical harm, pain, or mental anguish.

- **CASPER** means Certification and Survey Provider Enhanced Reporting.

- **Certification of Compliance** means that the SNF/NF is in at least substantial compliance and is therefore eligible to participate in Medicaid as a nursing facility, or in Medicare as a skilled nursing facility, or in both as a dually participating facility.

- **CFR** means Code of Federal Regulations.

- **CMP** means Civil Money Penalty.

- **CMS** means Centers for Medicare & Medicaid Services (formerly HCFA).

- **Deficiency** means that the skilled nursing facility or nursing facility failed to meet a participation requirement specified in the Act or in 42 CFR Part 483 Subpart B. (42 CFR 488.301)

- **Dual Participating Facility** means that the provider (SNF or NF) has an agreement in both the Medicare and Medicaid programs.

- **Educational program** means programs that include any subject pertaining to the long term care participating requirements, the survey process, of the enforcement process.

- **Enforcement action** means the process of imposing one or more of the remedies outlined in the second expectation by CMS: CMP, temporary manager, directed pan of correction, directed in-service training, denial of payment for new admission, state monitoring, transfer of residents, closure of facility and transfer of residents, or other CMS approved remedy.

- **Expanded survey** means an increase beyond the core task of a standard survey. This may come about when surveyors suspect substandard quality of care during a standard survey.

- **Facility** means a skilled nursing facility, or a distinct part of a skilled nursing facility, or nursing facility.

- **IDR** means Informal dispute resolution.

- **IJ** means Immediate Jeopardy. Immediate Jeopardy means a situation in which the facility's noncompliance with one or more requirements of participation has caused, or is likely to cause, serious injury, harm, impairment, or death to a resident.

- **Immediate family** means husband or wife; natural or adoptive parent, child or sibling, stepparent, stepchild, stepbrother, or stepsister, father-in-law, mother-in-law, son-in-law, daughter-in-law, brother-in-law, or sister-in-law, grandparent or grandchild.

- **LSC** means Life Safety Code.

- **Misappropriation of Resident Property** means the deliberate misplacement, exploitation, or wrongful, temporary or permanent use of a resident belongings or money without the resident's consent.

- **Neglect** means failure to provide good and services necessary to avoid physical harm, mental anguish, or mental illness.

- **Noncomplian**t means any deficiency that causes a facility not to be in substantial compliant.

- **No opportunity to correct** means that the facility will have remedies imposed immediately after determination of noncompliance has been made.

- **Nurse aide** means an individual providing nursing-related services to residents in accordance with 42CFR 483.75€ (1) CFR 42488.301.

- **Nursing facility** means a Medicaid nursing facility.

- **Opportunity to correct** means the facility is allowed an opportunity to correct identified deficiencies before remedies are imposed.

- **Past Noncompliance** means a deficiency citation at a specific survey data tag (F-tag or K-tag) that meets the following three criteria:

  - The facility was not in compliance with the specific regulatory requirement(s) at the time the situation occurred.

  - The noncompliance occurred after the exit date of the last standard (recertification) survey and before the currently being conducted survey.

  - There is sufficient evidence that the facility corrected the noncompliance and is in substantial compliance to the time of the current survey.

- **Per Day Civil Money Penalty** means a civil money penalty imposed for the number of days the facility was not in substantial compliance.

- **Per Instance Civil Money Penalty** means a civil money penalty imposed for each instance of facility noncompliance.

- **PoC** means Plan of Correction (42 CFR 488.401).

- **Representative** for purpose of educational program, means family members, legal guardians, friends, and ombudsmen assigned to the facility.

- **Self-Reported Noncompliance** means noncompliance that is reported by a facility to the State Survey Agency before it is identified by the State, CMS, or reported to the State or CMS by an entity other than the facility itself.

- **SFF** means Special Focus Facility.

- **Skilled nursing facility** means a Medicare-certified nursing facility that has a Medicare provider agreement.

- **SMA** means State Medicaid Agency, means the agency in the State that is responsible to administering the Medicaid program.

- **SNF** means skilled nursing facility.

- **SQC** mean substandard quality of care. This means one or more deficiencies related to participation requirements under 42CFR 483.13, resident behavior and facility practices, 42CFR 483.15, quality of life 42CFR 483.25, quality of care, that constitute either immediate jeopardy to resident health or safety, a pattern of widespread actual harm that is not immediate jeopardy, or a widespread potential for more than minimal harm, but less than immediate jeopardy, with no actual harm.

- **Standard survey** means periodic, resident-centered inspection that gathers information about the quality of service furnished to determine compliance with the requirement of participation (42CFR 488.301).

- **State Survey Agency (SA)** means the entity responsible for conducting most surveys to certify compliance with the Centers for Medicare and Medicaid Services' participation requirements.

- **Substantial compliance** means a level of compliance with the requirements of participation such that any identified deficiencies pose no greater risk to resident health or safety than the potential for causing minimal harm. Substantial compliance constitutes compliance with participation requirements. (42CFR 488.301)

ADDITIONAL DEFINITIONS

BELOW IS THE LISTING OF THE DIFFERENT type of Surveys conducted by the State and/or Federal surveyors on skilled nursing facilities and/or a nursing facilities. The State Survey Agency (SA) has responsibility for conducting most surveys and certifying compliance with the Centers for Medicare and Medicaid Services' participation requirements.

- **Initial Certification Survey**

    An initial survey must verify and validate substantial compliance with the regulatory requirements contained in the new reformed Federal long term care regulations and the specific State long term care regulations. Federal long term care regulations are contained in <u>42 CFR 483.5 through 42 CFR 483.75.</u>

- **Resurvey of Participating Facilities**

    For a resurvey the surveyors will follow the same protocol for a standard survey or for an extended survey. A resurvey is conducted by surveyors to validate that deficiencies have been corrected and implemented by the SNF/NF.

- **Post Survey Revisit (Follow-Up)**

    When the State surveyors have cited deficiencies on a facility during the course of a survey, the survey agency may, as necessary, conduct a post survey revisit to determine if the facility now meets the requirements for participation. The survey team will focus on those areas where the deficiencies were cited.

    It must be stressed here that while surveyors are in a facility for survey revisit, if they observe any quality of care issues or quality of life issues or any substandard practices that were never part of the original deficiencies, the surveyors will cite those issues as new deficiencies.

- **Abbreviated Standard Survey**

    This survey for the most part pertains to survey that focus on specific tasks that may relate to a complaint, or change in administrator or director of nursing, or change in

Management Company. This survey concentrates mainly on the areas of the complaint if it relates to compliant, not on all aspects of the regulations.

As is always stressed staffs need to be aware that when surveyors walk into a facility and observe troubling issues, they may extend the survey beyond the original intent.

- **Extended Survey/Partial Extended Survey**

    This survey is the result of observation(s) by surveyors during a standard survey or abbreviated standard survey, which has the potential for sub-standard quality of care outcome(s). When surveyors are conducting a standard survey or abbreviated standard survey, and they suspect sub-standard quality of care at the facility, then the survey will be extended.

- **State Monitoring Visits**

    These State Monitoring Visits are visits by the state to oversee a facility/provider's compliance status and are not done as part of enforcement remedy. These are visits that are done due to a facility that may be in bankruptcy, or a facility that may change ownership as authorized by a CMS regional office, or during or shortly after removal of an Immediate Jeopardy when the purpose of the visit is to ensure the welfare of the residents by providing an oversight presence.

- **Survey Frequency**

    Based on the survey and certification provision established, skilled nursing facilities and nursing facilities must be subject to a standard survey at minimum every 15 months after the last day of the previous standard survey, and that the statewide average interval between standard surveys not to exceed 12 months.

- **Last Day of Survey**

    The last day of a survey is the last day the surveyors were in the facility conducting onsite observation, regardless whether the surveyors did an exit conference on that same day or not.

    How to Count the three months and six months of the enforcement track when noncompliance is identified:

    If the health and life safety codes are on the same enforcement track, CMS uses the last day of the onsite observation of the standard health survey on which the noncompliance were identified. If the life safety was the second survey on the same enforcement track, and the noncompliance was found on the life safety, the clock starts ticking from the last day of onsite observation on the health survey.

When two enforcement tracks are being used (one track for the health portion and one track for life safety), the mandatory denial of payment for new admissions and termination time frames will be three and six months from each separate portion.

- **Setting the Mandatory 3-Month and 6-Month Sanction Time Frames**

    These dates are set based on full months rather than number of days. So the date will be set by going to the same numerical date in the 3rd or 6th month following the survey date. Example is, if a survey ended January 15, then the mandatory denial of payment for new admission remedy will be April 15, and the six-month mandatory termination will be July 15. For those calendar months that do not flow smoothly such as, if the last date of the survey was January 31, then the 3-Month clock will be May 1, as April only has 30 days, and the 6-month clock will be July 31.

- **Scheduling and Conducting Surveys**

    As stated above skilled nursing facilities and nursing facilities must have their standard surveys no later than every 15 months, with the state average not to exceed 12 months.

    The following changes in an organization or facility may prompt a survey sooner:

    - Change in ownership.

    - Change in management firm.

    - Change in Administrator.

    - Change in Director of nursing.

    Facilities with history of poor performance may be surveyed more frequently to ensure that residents are receiving quality of care in a safe environment.

    Complaint(s) received may prompt an abbreviated survey.

- **Unannounced Surveys**

    CMS policy mandates that all skilled nursing facilities and nursing facilities surveys must be unannounced, whether they are standard surveys, complaint surveys, and onsite revisit surveys. The State must not only keep the survey unannounced, they must also ensure that the timing of the survey is unpredictable. Also if the CMS conducts standard survey or validation survey, the regional office must also follow the same protocol and keep the survey unannounced. An exception to this protocol is that the State should notify the Ombudsman's office of the survey but must hold the Ombudsman's office to strict confidentiality concerning the survey dates.

- **Informal Dispute Resolution**

    The regulations require that CMS and the States offer the skilled nursing facilities, the nursing facilities, and the dually certified facilities an informal opportunity to dispute cited deficiencies upon the facility's receipt of the official Form CMS-2567. State should send the notice of the Informal Dispute Resolution (IDR) and the process, with the letter that is sent to the facility with the Form CMS-2567. The notification should inform the facility:

    - That it may request the opportunity for informal dispute resolution (IDR), and that this request must be made within the same 10 calendar day period the facility has for submitting an acceptable plan of correction to the survey entity.

    - Of the name, address, and telephone number of the person the facility must contact to request the IDR.

    - How IDR may be accomplished in that State, e.g. by telephone, in writing, or in face-to-face.

    - Of the name or position/title of the person who will be conducting the IDR.

IDR process is an opportunity that facilities must take advantage of, but CMS requires that this process must not be used to delay the imposition of remedies. The IDR must also not be used by facilities to challenge the scope and severity of deficiencies except if the scope and severity is for a substandard quality of care or an immediate jeopardy.

When a facility is unsuccessful in its IDR, the survey entity must inform the facility in writing that it was unsuccessful. When a facility is successful in its IDR process at demonstrating that a deficiency should not have been cited, or that a scope and severity should be adjusted based on CMS policy, the State survey agency manager will sign and date the revised CMS Form-2567. The facility also has the option to request a clean or new CMS Form-2567.

For revisit surveys, IDR may be requested based on the result of the revisit or based on the result of the previous IDR outcome. Facilities are eligible to request a IDR for a revisit if the deficiency is a continuation of the same deficiency at revisit, if new deficiency is cited, or new instance of deficiency. A facility may not request IDR for a revisit if a different tag is cited but the same facts, except if the new tag constitute a substandard quality of care.

CMS encourages States to include one person in the IDR decision making process, who was not directly involved in the survey.

- **Independent Informal Dispute Resolution (Independent IDR)**

    The regulation requires that SNFs, NFs, SNFs/NFs are provided the opportunity to request and participate in an independent IDR if CMS imposes civil monetary penalties (CMP) against the facility and these penalties are collected and subject to be placed in an escrow account pending administrative decisions. Actually all CMP funds are subject to be placed in escrow.

    - An opportunity for an independent IDR is provided within 30 days of the imposition of the civil monetary penalty.

    - The facility must request an Independent IDR within 10 calendar days of receipt of the offer.

    - The CMS Regional Office will communicate the offer for the Independent IDR in its initial Notice of Imposition of a Penalty letter to the facility.

    - The CMS notice will include the State survey agency contact information, including the name, address, and telephone number of the person that the facility must contact to request the Independent IDR.

    - An independent IDR should be completed as soon as practicable but not later than 60 days of the facility's request if the request is made timely.

    - An independent IDR will be approved by CMS and conducted by the State.

SURVEY PROCESS

THE ADMINISTRATOR, HAVING RESPONSIBILITY FOR THE OVERALL management of the facility and the Director of Nursing, having responsibility for the nursing department and nursing functions, are usually the key members of the facility leadership team who are "front and center" and heavily involved in all aspects of the survey process. Almost everyone in the long term care community is now aware that there is a new survey process, which is a combination of both the former Traditional and QIS surveys. CMS set out to build on the best of both the Traditional and QIS survey processes to establish a single nationwide survey process, with the goals of efficiency and effectiveness, as well as a goal of being resident-centered. All surveys are of course unannounced and the standard survey has a frequency of 15-Month Interval and 12-Month State-wide Average. In addition to annual surveys facilities undergo complaint surveys, and there are other surveys that may be triggered by change in ownership, change in management, or change in administrator or director of nursing, or facilities may also undergo more frequent surveys due to poor histories of compliance.

The new survey process has mandatory offsite preparation by the Survey Team Coordinator (TC) or Team Leader. The survey team should and usually include registered nurses, registered dietitians, pharmacists, social workers, activity professionals, or rehabilitative specialists when possible. With the new survey process, each survey team member uses a tablet or laptop PC throughout the survey process to record findings that are synthesized and organized by new software. To prepare for the survey, the Team Coordinator will make specific mandatory assignments for the survey team members upon entry into the facility. Surveyors' entrance assignments will include:[5]

- Immediate visit to the Kitchen for observation of the kitchen.

- Resident Dining Observation of the resident's full meal after entrance into the facility.

- Infection Control–relative to the kitchen and food service workers.

- Sufficient and Competent Nurse Staffing.

---

[5]   www.CMS.gov/Medicare/Provider-Enrollment-and-Certification/Guidancefor LawsAndRegulations…

Other mandatory entrance assignments include:

- Medication Administration
- Medication Storage
- Resident Council Meeting and
- Beneficiary Protection Notification Review.

The new survey process requires that the Team Coordinator have a brief entrance meeting with the facility administrator and the Director of Nursing. If the administrator and director of nursing are not present at the facility when the surveyors arrive, then someone in leadership will sit in for the administrator and meet with the Team Coordinator. While the TC is meeting with the administrator, the other members of the survey team will go immediately to their assigned areas when they enter the facility. As stated above one of those assigned areas is the kitchen. So Food Service Director or Kitchen Supervisor must be familiar with the survey process to help their staff know what the expectations are from the surveyors. The surveyor assigned to the kitchen will conduct an initial brief visit to the kitchen and will utilize a kitchen observation tool to record his/her observation findings. Based on my experience, the surveyor doing the kitchen observation will usually ask the Food Service Director or Supervisor an important question. The surveyor's question usually will be: "Is there or are there any issues in the kitchen that I (surveyor) need to be aware of?" As someone who has had many years' experience with surveyors, I believe the reason for this question could be at least twofold:

- One is, the surveyor may want to know whether the director or supervisor is aware of what is going on in their foodservice department or in the kitchen.

- Two is, the surveyor may want to know whether the director or supervisor is giving good accurate information to him/her.

If there are some serious issue(s) going on that the director or supervisor did not disclose to the surveyor, and the surveyor found out during observation of the kitchen, then this becomes a serious matter of noncompliance. It is better for the food service manager/supervisor to disclose issues/problems and let the surveyors know that the facility is aware and working on the solution, than to not disclose. Because the kitchen is one of the most important locations in the facility/building, the administrator and food service director must ensure that the kitchen meets regulatory compliance at all times. Below are some areas that the surveyor will observe during the initial kitchen observation:

- The freezer and the walk-in refrigerator–are the freezer and walk-in refrigerator working properly and maintaining the required temperatures? Are there temperature logs that staff records daily temperature readings?

- Are food items in the walk-in refrigerator(s) labelled and dated?

- Is there outdated food in the refrigerator(s)?

- For the dishwashing machine, is the wash cycle and rinse cycle for the dishwashing machine maintaining the required temperatures? Is there a temperature log? The temperature log must have record of after breakfast, after lunch, and after diner temperature readings.

- For food handling and food preparation–Is food prepared, cooked, or stored under appropriate temperatures.

- Also is food handled, prepared, and distributed in a manner that prevents foodborne illness to the residents?

- Is potentially hazardous food, such as meat, chicken, pork sitting on top of the counter thawing at room temperature?

- The cleanliness of the kitchen.

- Do staff wear hair net and appropriate head coverings.

- Infection control–is there a sink for handwashing, and is staff using proper hand washing and hand hygiene technique.

- For Food Service–does the facility have a qualified dietitian or qualified nutritional professional?

WHEN SURVEYORS WALK THROUGH YOUR DOORS

Let us say that the survey is for an annual certification survey. Below is a list of processes the surveyors will embark on. The administrator, director of nursing, department directors, QAPI director, staff development director or coordinator and nursing supervisors will need to have familiarity with this process.

- **Offsite Preparation by surveyors** is mainly the work of the survey team coordinator (TC). Mandatory facility tasks assignments for the survey team are done by the TC. The TC reviews the CASPER 3 Report to determine the previous survey deficiencies for prior Annual Surveys and Complaint Surveys, and more importantly to determine the pattern of deficiencies. The TC also contacts the ombudsman to inform the ombudsman in confidence of the upcoming survey, and to find out any information or concerns the ombudsman may have about the facility.

- **Facility Entrance**—all members of the survey team go to their assigned areas, except the team coordinator will meet with the administrator for a brief entrance conference. One surveyor will go directly to the kitchen to do initial observation, and ask questions of supervisor and staff as has already been noted. The TC will need from the administrator or designee if administrator is unavailable when the survey team walks into the facility the items listed below. If the administrator is unavailable, the director of nursing will usually do the brief entrance conference. The TC will request from the administrator the following documents immediately:

    1. Census number.

    2. Complete matrix for new admission in the last 30 days who are residing in the facility.

    3. An alphabetical list of all residents (note residents who are out of the facility).

    4. A list of residents who smoke, designated smoking times, and locations.

- **Entrance Conference Worksheet**–The Food Service Director or supervisor should be aware that the surveyor will request through the administrator the following documents within one hour of entrance: (1) the schedule of meal times, (2) locations of dining rooms, (3) copies of all current menus including therapeutic menus that will be served for the duration of the survey and (4) the policy and procedure for food brought in from visitors. Also needed within one hour of entrance is a list of paid feeding assistants if the facility employs paid feeding assistant, also information about whether the paid feeding assistant completed their training through the state approved training program, a list of residents who are eligible for assistance and who are currently receiving assistance from paid feeding assistants. The Director of nursing will provide information on paid feeding assistants, if applicable, for the administrator. Document on the Infection Prevention and Control Program Standards, Policies and Procedures, and Antibiotic Stewardship Program is required within 4 hours of entrance.

  There are occasions when a survey is an off-hour survey, meaning surveyors show up during non-business hours. If the survey is an off-hour survey, the TC will conduct the entrance conference with the person in charge, and the TC will conduct a conference if needed with the administrator when he/she arrives. During off-hours, the person in charge is usually the nursing supervisor.

  An important recommendation is for facilities to utilize the Entrance Conference Worksheet to complete and compile all the information needed by the surveyors and maintain these documents in a binder, usually named a "survey binder". It is also advisable to have duplicate survey binder, so one can be kept in the administrator's office and the second binder kept for the nursing supervisor, so administrators, when surveyors walk into your facilities you and your team will be prepared and you will have the needed documents within the required timeframe. As surveys are unannounced, the documents should be updated because the documents are time sensitive.

Below is the list of documents requested in the Entrance Conference Worksheet. This form can be downloaded from the CMS or related or affiliated website.

ENTRANCE CONFERENCE WORKSHEET[6]

- **Information Needed from the Facility Immediately upon Entrance**

    1. Census number.

    2. Complete matrix for new admission in the last 30 days who are still residing in the facility.

    3. An alphabetical list of all residents (note any resident out of the facility).

    4. A list of residents who smoke, designated smoking times, and locations.

- **Entrance Conference**

    5. Conduct a brief Entrance Conference with the Administrator.

    6. Information regarding full time DON coverage (verbal confirmation is acceptable).

    7. Information about the facility's emergency water sauce (verbal confirmation is acceptable).

    8. Signs announcing the survey that are posted in high-visibility areas.

    9. A copy of an updated facility floor plan, if changes have been made.

    10. Name of Resident Council President.

    11. Provide the facility with a copy of the CASPER 3.

---

6   CMS Compliance Group, Inc. Blog New LTC Survey Pathways & Entrance Conference Form page 3.

- **Information Needed From Facility Within One Hour of Entrance**

    12. Schedule of meal times, locations of dining rooms, copies of all current menus including therapeutic menus that will be served for the duration of the survey and the policy for food brought in from visitors.

    13. Schedule of Medication Administration times.

    14. Number and location of med storage rooms and med carts.

    15. The actual working schedules for licensed and registered nursing staff for the survey time period.

    16. List of key personnel, location, and phone numbers. Note contract staff (e.g. rehab services).

    17. If the facility employs paid feeding assistants, provide the following information.

        a. Whether the paid feeding assistant training was provided through a State-approved training program by qualified professionals as defined by State law, with minimum of 8 hours of training.

        b. Names of staff (including agency staff) who have successfully completed training for paid feeding assistants, and who are currently assisting selected residents with eating meals and/or snacks.

        c. A list of residents who are eligible for assistance and who are currently receiving assistance from paid feeding assistants.

- **Information Needed From Facility within Four Hours of Entrance**

    18. Complete the matrix for all other residents. The TC confirms the matrix was completed accurately.

    19. Admission packet.

    20. Dialysis Contract(s), Agreement(s), Arrangement(s), and Policy and Procedures, if applicable.

21. List of qualified staff providing hemodialysis or assistance for peritoneal dialysis treatments, if applicable.

22. Agreement(s) or Policies and Procedures for transport to and from dialysis treatments, if applicable.

23. Does the facility have an onsite separately certified ESRD unit?

24. Hospice Agreement, and Policies and Procedures for each hospice used (name of facility designee(s) who coordinate(s) services with hospice provider(s).

25. Infection Prevention and Control Program Standards, Policies and Procedures, and Antibiotic Stewardship Program.

26. Influenza / Pneumococcal Immunization Policy & Procedures.

27. QAA committee information (name of contact, names of members and frequency of meetings).

28. QAPI Plan.

29. Abuse Prohibition Policy and Procedures.

30. Description of any experimental research occurring in the facility.

31. Facility assessment.

32. Nurse staffing waivers.

33. List of rooms meeting one of the following conditions that require a variance:

    a. Less than the required square footage.

    b. More than four residents.

- **Information Needed By The End of the First Day of Survey**

    34. Provide each surveyor with access to all resident electronic records –do not exclude any information that should be a part of the resident's medical record. Provide specific information on how surveyors can access the EHRs outside of the conference room.

Please complete the attached form on page 4 which is titled "Electronic Health Record Information".

- **Information Needed From Facility Within 24 Hours of Entrance**

    35. Completed Medicare/Medicaid Application (CMS-671).

    36. Completed Census and Condition Information (CMS-672).

    37. Please complete the attached form on Page 3 which is titled "Beneficiary Notice–Residents Discharged Within the Last Six Months.

Survey Process continued:

Screening

Surveyors will follow their assignments and go to their assigned units or floors to do an initial brief screening or quick observing of the residents and the environment. Surveyors will ask for resident rosters for their assigned areas. The surveyors will go room to room on the units without staff accompanying them. Surveyors will observe the residents from head to toe. They (surveyors) will spend the first eight to ten hours completing the initial pool, which entails screening residents, observation, interview residents if appropriate, and limited record review of the initial pool residents. During the quick observation, if the surveyors identify some concern(s), they will ask the resident(s) brief question(s) to make determination of potential issues or problems. The initial pool residents usually comprise, offsite selected residents that are in the facility, active complaint, and the team's on-site selected residents which include vulnerable residents, new admissions, or identified concerns.

Review the Matrix

Surveyors will review the matrix of residents in their assigned area to identify any substantial concern that should be followed-up. Surveyors will cover every care area for interviewable residents to determine if any care area(s) warrants further investigation or if there are no issues. Concerning Nutrition, the surveyor that has responsibility for that care area, will utilize his/her weight calculator to calculate weight loss/gain. For non-interviewable residents in the initial pool, the resident representative or family will be contacted on day one of the survey to conduct an interview to ascertain if the family or representative has concern(s). The surveyors will ask questions on all care areas and get responses to the resident interview or resident representative or family interview.

If a surveyor identifies a significant major concern during observations, interview, or limited record review, the surveyor will identify that as Immediate Jeopardy (IJ) or harm if that is potentially the case, and the survey team will meet immediately to confer and discuss the matter. **Immediate Jeopardy is defined as a situation in which the facility's failure to meet one or more requirements of participation has caused, or is likely to cause, serious injury, harm, impairment, or death to a resident.**[7] If the survey team confirms that the situation is potentially an IJ, the TC will immediately inform his/her supervisor. If the supervisor concurs that the situation constitutes immediate jeopardy, the team coordinator immediately informs the administrator or designee of the presence of an IJ. The administrator and his/her team will begin to take immediate action to remove the IJ. It is strongly recommended that if a facility has the unfortunate occurrence of an Immediate Jeopardy during a survey, the administrator and his/her team must work very hard and do everything within their powers to have the IJ removed prior to the end of the survey.

Dining Observation

All surveyors will complete dining observations on day one, the first Full meal after their entrance. The team should cover dining locations and room trays as well. Surveyors will cover enough of the residents' dining experience to identify issues or concerns. Surveyors will observe dining experience of residents with MDS indicator of weight loss, food or hydration concern. If concerns are identified during dining experience observation, there will be a second full meal dining observation.

Infection Control

During the tours all surveyors will observe for break in infection control protocol by staffs. In addition, the surveyor assigned for infection prevention and control, other surveyors will review the infection prevention and control program and antibiotic stewardship program, the influenza and pneumococcal vaccinations.

SNF Beneficiary Protection Notification Review

There will be a random selection of three residents from the list provided on the Entrance Conference Form.

Kitchen

Surveyors will make observations of the kitchen throughout the survey and gather needed information. Unit refrigerators are considered part of the kitchen process, so surveyor will observe temperatures of refrigerators on the nursing units to ensure proper temperatures are maintained.

---

7   Long Term Care Survey Process Procedure Guide Effective May 5, 2019, page 26.

Medication Administration

The nurse surveyor and/or the pharmacist surveyor will observe medication administration for either sampled residents or for any resident that the nurse is ready to administer meds. The surveyor will observe different routes, different units and different shifts. The survey process requires that 25 medication opportunities be observed. The Nurse surveyor and/or pharmacist surveyor will also observe if any expired meds were administered to residents. Med error rate will be determined if any.

Med Storage

Surveyors will look at med storage rooms on half the units and med carts on half of the other units. If there are no concerns then observation is complete, but if there are concerns, then the surveyors will expand the review.

Resident Council Meeting

The surveyor assigned will complete an interview with the resident council president and review three months' worth of minutes of the meetings to determine if there are any concerns and whether those issues are unresolved. This interview will most likely be done on day two of the survey.

Environment

Surveyors will review those areas that surveyors have concerns about. For the environment observation, surveyors do not have to review oxygen storage, the generator, or the Emergency Preparedness as these areas fall under Life Safety Code, and will be covered when the life safety code survey is done.

Sufficient and Competent Nurse Staffing

Throughout the survey, the surveyors are considering whether staffing can be linked to residents or family complaints, whether staffing can be linked to quality of care or quality of life issues or concerns observed. Surveyors will also review facility complaint log and some completed complaints received by the facility as part of the facility's complaint process. Surveyors also usually ask for staffing schedule for licensed nurses and nursing aides or certified nursing assistants during the survey period.

Personal Funds

This review is completed if there are complaints that residents do not have access to their funds or that residents are not receiving their quarterly statements.

Resident Assessment

If the surveyor identifies discrepancy concerns with the MDS, e.g. delay with completion and/or submission of the MDS, the surveyor will complete a review of resident assessment in the care area.

Substandard Quality of Care (SQC) and Extended Survey

If substandard quality of care issue(s) is/are identified by any one surveyor, the team will complete an extended survey. Substandard quality of care can be identified and a determination made at any point during the survey if SQC exist in the facility.

End of Day Meeting

Each surveyor will share his/her data with the survey Team Coordinator prior to the team meeting. The team will have brief daily end of day meetings when they will review their notes and findings.

Quality Assessment & Assurance (QAA)/Quality Assurance Performance Improvement (QAPI)

This is usually one of the final stages of the survey. The TC will ask the QAPI director responsible for the QAPI program, for the facility's QAPI plan. At this point the TC will ask the QAPI director what areas of quality or performance improvement the facility is working on. The size of the facility, the number of beds, and the quality issues identified usually determines how long the surveyors will be at the facility.

Critical Elements

The survey team has a list of care areas that are identified as critical elements that is part of the new survey process. The surveyors utilize these critical elements process to review the care areas to identify whether standard of care protocols are being met, and whether there are serious or major areas of concerns that may later become potential citations and deficiencies for the facility.

Determination of Deficient Practices

The team will have a final meeting to share data with each other and the Team Coordinator; and also to ensure that the investigation of all areas is complete. The TC and the team will come to a determination as to what areas of the regulation and F-tags meet compliance and which do not; which F-tags will have a deficiency citation and which F-tags will not.

Exit Conference

This is the final stage of the on-site survey process. The TC will inform the administrator that they have come to the end of the survey and give the administrator an estimated time of the day when he/she will like to meet with the administrator and his/her leadership team to go over findings. It must be stressed here that the intent for the exit conference is for the survey team to inform the facility of the survey team's observations and preliminary findings. The TC will give the administrator a list of the residents in the survey sample with corresponding identifying numbers because residents' identity cannot be disclosed. The TC will give the facility opportunity to provide additional information that they believe is pertinent to the issue that is being discussed. The TC will reinforce again that the exit conference is a preliminary deficiency findings meeting/conference and that the administrator will receive a survey report, Form CMS-2567 which contains the deficiencies that have been cited. After facilities receive their Form CMS-2567, the facility has ten consecutive days to submit their response to the survey agency.

It must also be noted here that if the survey is an annual health certification survey, the facility will also receive a Life Safety Code survey either soon before the certification survey or soon thereafter.

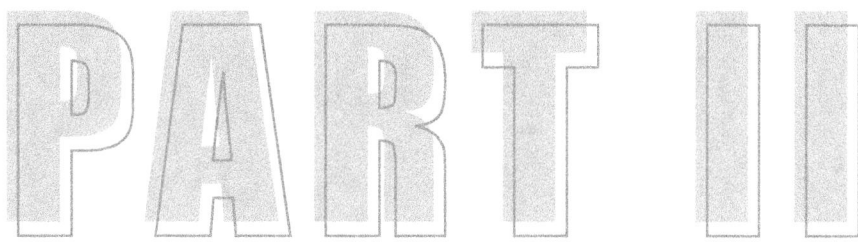

REVISED REGULATIONS WITH NEW F-TAGS

AND

MONITORING TOOLS

RESIDENT MEAL TIME & DINING EXPERIENCE

KITCHEN & FOOD SERVICE

§483.60–FOOD AND NUTRITION SERVICES; ETC.

NEW F-TAGS

These are the revised or reform Federal Long Term Care Regulations with an effective date of November 28, 2017. F-Tags and regulations listed and formatted for easy reading and easy following so staff can make quick references to the regulations when needed while they provide care for the residents. This will help staff increase their familiarity with the regulations to improve quality of care and quality life for the residents they serve. I recommend that copies of this book be placed at the nurses' station for easy access for nurse managers, charge nurses and certified nursing assistants or nurse aides, for dietitian, and also for the food service manager/director and food service staff. In addition to the regulations highlighted, I have included comments and statements reinforcing important points I believe need to be stressed, intent about some of the regulations, and some of the surveyor interpretive guidance of the regulations.

HOW TO USE THE MONITORING TOOLS

The Monitoring Tools for Resident Meal Time & Dining Experience and Kitchen & Food Service are designed in an easy-to-read and easy-to-follow format. The monitoring tools reflect the current Federal Long Term Care Regulations, the Interpretive Guidelines and the author's comments and statements based on her expertise and experience as a twenty-seven plus years as a hands-on nursing home administrator. Staffs should utilize these tools to help embrace the habit of regular ongoing monitoring for quality and regulatory compliance, as well as utilize the tools for survey preparedness. These tools are easy to follow, easy to utilize for daily, weekly and/or monthly monitoring. Results of the monitoring can be incorporated into your facilities' QAPI program for analysis of compliance outcomes.

It is a good practice to have interdisciplinary teams work together to observe resident meals. The team can observe staff response and response time when food carts are delivered to the floors or the units. They can observe whether the staffs make themselves available to serve the residents their meals, or whether the food stays unattended in the food service delivery cart for a long time. They can also observe staffs' interaction with the residents during meal time. If the facility has paid feeding assistants, are the paid feeding assistants working under the supervision of a Licensed Practical Nurse or a Registered Nurse? The facility will decide if they want to use teams to do the internal observation/monitoring or if they prefer individual staff members to do the observation or monitoring. It is the administrator's, DON's or QA Director's choice if they use teams or individual staff persons.

Monitoring of the kitchen can also be done by an interdisciplinary team if the facility so chooses. The facility can put their own internal teams together comprising the Director or Manager of Food Service, the Facility/Maintenance Director, Quality Assurance Director, Food Service Supervisor, and the Administrator to do a walk-through and observe the kitchen and the food service staff for compliance. In addition to utilizing these monitoring tools the teams must also have available the State Dietary Manual, and other State requirements for food service. The staffs doing the internal monitoring must check freezer and refrigerators temperatures to ensure that the food is maintained at the proper temperature. All areas of the kitchen must be observed for compliance on a regular daily or weekly basis, because a surveyor is assigned to the kitchen as one of the first places in the facility upon entrance for a survey.

Long Term Care Monitoring for Quality
Resident Meal Time Food and Nutrition Services Revised

Facilities must remember that one of CMS' expectations for SNFs and NFs is routine consistent monitoring of their performance for quality in order to stay in substantial compliance of the requirements of participation in the Medicare & Medicaid programs.

The key for the monitoring tools are as follows:

Y–Yes
N–No
NA–Not Applicable

REGULATIONS & F-TAGS FOR RESIDENT MEAL TIME AND DINING EXPERIENCE

LISTING OF THE CFR AND THE TAG **Title relevant to the above topic focus:**

42 CFR §483.10(a): "Resident Rights: The resident has a right to a dignified existence, self-determination, and communication with and access to persons inside and outside the facility".

§483.10(i)((1)-(7): Safe, clean, comfortable, and homelike Environment, including comfortable lighting, safe temperature levels, comfortable sound levels.

§483.20(a): Admissions Orders–physician order for resident's immediate care upon admission.

§483.24: Quality of Life.

§483.24(a)1)(b)(1)-(5)(i)(iii): Activities of Daily Living (ADLs)/ Maintain Abilities.

§483.24(a)(2): ADL Care Provided for Dependent Residents.

§483.25(g)(1)-(3): Nutrition/Hydration Status Maintenance.

§483.60: Provided Diet Meets Needs of Each Resident.

§483.60(a)(1)(2): Qualified Dietary Staff.

§483.60(a)(3)(b): Sufficient Dietary Support Personnel.

§483.60(c)(1)-(7): Menus Meet Res Needs/Prep in Advance/Followed.

§483.60(d)(1)(2): Nutritive Value/Appear, Palatable/Prefer Temp.

§483.60(d)(3): Food in Form to Meet Individual Needs.

§483.60(d)(4)(5): Resident Allergies, Preferences and Substitutes.

§483.60(d)(6): Drinks Available to Meet Needs/Preferences/Hydration.

§483.60(e)(1)(2): Therapeutic Diets Prescribed by Physician.

§483.60(f)(1)-(3): Frequency of Meals/Snacks at Bedtime.

§483.60(g): Assistive Devices–Eating Equipment/Utensils.

§483.60(h)(1)-(3): Feeding Assistants –Training/Supervision/Resident.

§483.60(i)(1)(2): Food Procurement; Store/Prepare/Serve –Sanitary.

§483.80(a)(1)(2)(4)(e)(f): Infection Prevention & Control.

§483.90(h)(1)-(4): Requirements for Dining and Activity Rooms.

§483.95(g)(1)-(4): Required In-Service Training for Nurse Aides.

§483.95(h): Training for Feeding Assistants.

The New F-Tags and Reform Regulations

The list below gives staff a quick easy-to-read and easy-to-follow version of the Reform Federal Long Term Care Regulations with related F-tags for those F-tags including Resident Rights, Food and Nutrition Services, etc. Included also are comments and statements of important aspects of the respective regulations to help staff focus on areas to increase and improve staff internalization and familiarity with the regulations for Quality of Care, Quality of Life, and Safety of the Environment of the residents in our skilled nursing facilities, nursing facilities, nursing homes and other long term care facilities. As you can see there are occasions when writing this book, I use the words "us" or "our", because I see myself as part of community, which I am. I am part of you, and understand full well the challenges, and also that feeling of intrinsic reward of helping residents and their families.

F550–Resident Rights:

The resident has a right to a dignified existence, self-determination, and communication with access to persons and services inside and outside the facility. A Facility staff must treat residents with respect and dignity and, while providing care for residents the staff must care for

each resident in a manner and in an environment that promotes maintenance or enhancement of each resident's Quality of Life, recognizing each resident's individuality.

Comments and Statements

Although this F-Tag is part of the Resident Rights regulation, it also addresses Resident Meal Time & Dining Experience, as well as Kitchen & Food Service. It is the expectation of the Federal and State governments that staffs treat residents with dignity and respect while providing care and services for residents. Also staff must assist residents in maintaining and enhancing their self-esteem and self-worth and incorporate the resident's goals, preferences, and choices.

For resident's meal time, (1) staff must treat residents with dignity by assisting residents as is reasonably possible to dress in their own clothes rather than hospital type gowns, (2) facility Food Service Department must avoid daily use of disposable plates and cutlery, (3) by having nurse aides or feeding assistants (as appropriate and approved) sit beside residents (not stand) while assisting residents to eat, and (4) having staff interact/talk to resident while assisting resident with meal as oppose to talking to other staff persons across the room.

Regulatory grouping for this F-tag is Resident Rights §483.10.

F584–Resident Rights–Safe Environment:

The resident has a Right to a safe, clean, comfortable and homelike environment, including treatment and support for the residents daily living safely. This includes residents' environment:

- **Being as homelike as much as possible.**

- **Having adequate and comfortable lighting levels.**

- **Having comfortable and safe temperature levels.**

- **Having and maintaining comfortable sound levels.**

Comments and Statements

In the common area such as the dining room where the residents eat their meals, the environment must be safe, lighting must be good, sound levels also must be good, and the temperature level must be within the required limits.

Regulatory Grouping for this F-tag is Resident Rights §483.10.

F635–Admissions Physician Orders for Immediate Care:

At the time resident is admitted, each resident must have physician order either written or verbal orders for his/her immediate care.

Comments/Statements

The importance of this regulation is to make sure that the resident receives the necessary and required care and services upon admission. The physician order must include at minimum dietary, medications if necessary and routine care to maintain or improve the resident's functional abilities until the staff conducts comprehensive assessment and develop the interdisciplinary care plan. The order can be written and/or verbal orders.

Regulatory Grouping for the F-tag is Resident Assessment §483.20.

F675–Quality of Life

Quality of Life is a fundamental principle that applies to all care and services provided to facility residents. Each resident must receive and the facility must provide the necessary care and services to attain or maintain the highest practicable physical, mental, and psychosocial well-being, consistent with the resident's comprehensive assessment and plan of care.

The intent of this regulation is to ensure that facility takes responsibility to create and sustain an environment that humanizes and individualizes each resident's quality of life:

- Ensuring all staff, across all shifts and departments, understand the principles of quality of life and supports these principles for each resident; and

- Ensuring that the care and services provided are person-centered, and honor and support each resident's preferences, choices, values, and beliefs.

Person-Centered Care is defined as the focus on the resident as the locus of control and support the resident in making their own choices and having control over their daily lives.

Quality of Life is defined as an individual's "sense of well-being, level of satisfaction with life and feeling of self-worth and self-esteem. For nursing home residents, this includes a basic sense of satisfaction with oneself, the environment, the care received, the accomplishments of desired goals, and control over one's life."

Comments and Statements

CMS is placing the onus on the administrator and other facility leadership to create an environment that humanizes and promotes each resident's well being, and feeling of self worth and self esteem. This requires SNFs/NFs and nursing home leadership to establish a culture within their facilities that treats each resident with dignity and respect as individuals and also to support the resident's feeling of self-worth including personal control over choices, such as mealtimes, activities, clothing, and bed-time, etc. Facility leadership must be aware of the culture that exist in their facilities, so as to be able to make corrections and culture change as needed, to uphold the intent of this regulation.

Regulatory Grouping for this F-tag is Quality of Life §483.24.

F676–Comprehensive Assessment of a resident consistent with resident's needs and choices.

Based on the comprehensive assessment of the resident and consistent with resident's choices and needs, the facility must provide the necessary care and services to ensure that the resident's abilities in activities of daily living (ADL) do not diminish unless circumstances of the individual clinical condition demonstrate that diminution was unavoidable; this includes that a resident is given the appropriate treatment and services to maintain or improve his or her ability to carry out the activities of daily living.

This also includes:

- **Hygiene –bathing, dressing, grooming, and oral care.**
- **Mobility –transfer and ambulation, including walking.**
- **Elimination –toileting.**
- **Dining –eating, including meals and snacks.**
- **Communication, including**
    - Speech
    - Language
    - Other functional communication systems.

Regulatory Grouping for this F-tag is Quality of Life §483.24.

F677–ADL Care Provided for Dependent Residents

A resident who is unable to carry out activities of daily living receives the necessary services to maintain good nutrition, grooming, and personal and oral hygiene.

Comments/Statement

It is understandable that residents have clinical diagnoses during their course of stay at the facility, but CMS does not expect that the existence of a clinical diagnosis to necessarily justify the residents decline in activities of daily living (ADLs), unless if the resident's clinical picture reflects the normal progression of the disease/condition which may result in an unavoidable decline in the resident's ability to perform ADLs. If a resident refuses care, the resident and/or responsible party must be informed and they should be educated about the risk of the refusal and also be offered possible alternatives; and there must be adequate documentation by nursing/IDT in the resident's care plan of other interventions made to help provide care for the resident, or efforts made to provide care for the resident.

Regulatory Grouping for this F-tag is of Quality of Life §483.24.

F692–Nutrition / Hydration Status Maintenance; Assisted nutrition and hydration Based on a resident's comprehensive assessment, the facility must ensure that a resident:

- **Maintain acceptable parameters of nutritional status such as usual body weight or desirable body weight range and electrolyte balance, unless the resident's clinical condition demonstrates that this is not possible or resident preferences indicate otherwise;**

- **Is offered sufficient fluid intake to maintain proper hydration and health;**

- **Is offered a therapeutic diet when there is a nutritional problem and the health care provider orders a therapeutic diet.**

Comments/Statements

CMS' intent for this regulation is that the resident maintains, to the extent possible, acceptable parameters of nutritional and hydration status and that the facility:

- Provides nutritional and hydration care and services to each resident, consistent with the resident's comprehensive assessment.

- Recognizes, evaluates and addresses the needs of every resident, including but not limited to, the resident at risk or already experiencing impaired and hydration; and

- Provides a therapeutic diet that takes into account the resident's clinical condition, and preferences, when there is a nutritional indication.

The regulation includes in its guidance, the importance for facilities to maintain the nutritional status of the residents to ensure that that each resident is able to maintain his or her highest practicable level of well-being. Interdisciplinary team members need to identify early enough those residents who at risk for impaired nutrition or hydration status, so the team can develop and implement interventions to stabilize or improve the resident's nutritional status before complication arise.

Below are Definitions per the regulation for the following clinical terms:

"Acceptable parameters of nutritional status" refers to factors that reflect that an individual's nutritional status is adequate, relative to his/her overall condition and prognosis, such as weight, food/fluid intake, and pertinent laboratory values.

"Artificial nutrition and hydration' are medical treatments and refer to nutrition that is provided through routes other than the usual oral route, typically by placing a tube directly into the stomach, the intestine or a vein.

"Clinically significant" refers to effects, results, or consequences that materially affect or are likely to affect an individual's physical, mental, or psychosocial well-being either positively by preventing, stabilizing, or improving a condition or reducing a risk, or negatively by exacerbating, causing, or contributing to a symptom, illness, or decline in status.

"Dietary supplements" refers to herbal and alternative products that are not regulated by the Food and Drug Administration and their composition is not standardized. Dietary supplements must be labeled as such and must not be represented for use as a conventional food or as the sole item of a meal or the diet.

"Health Care Provider" as defined in this section by CMS includes a physician, physician assistant, nurse practitioner, or clinical nurse specialist, or a qualified dietitian or **other nutrition professional acting within their state scope of practice and to whom the attending physician has delegated the task.**

"Nutritional Supplements" refers to products that are used to complement a resident's dietary needs (e.g. calorie or nutrient dense drinks, total parenteral products, and meal replacement products).

"Therapeutic diet" refers to a diet ordered by a physician or other delegated provider that is part of the treatment for a disease or clinical condition, to eliminate, decrease, or increase certain substances in the diet (e.g. sodium or potassium), or to provide mechanically altered food when indicated.

"Tube feeding" refers to the delivery of nutrients through a feeding tube directly into the stomach duodenum, or jejunum. It is also referred to as an enteral feeding.

Suggested parameters for evaluating significance of unplanned and undesired weight loss are:

Interval	Significant Loss	Severe Loss
1 Month	5%	Greater than 5%
3 Months	7.5%	Greater than 7.5%
6 Months	10%	Greater than 10%

It is recommended that a comprehensive nutritional assessment should be completed on any resident identified as being at risk for unplanned weight loss/gain and/or compromised nutritional status. Through the comprehensive assessment the IDT will clarify nutritional issues, needs and goals in relation to the resident's overall condition.

The current professional standards of practice recommend weighing the resident on admission or readmission (to establish a baseline weight), weekly for the first 4 weeks after admission and at least monthly thereafter to help identify and document trends such as slow or progressive weight loss.

The information gathered from the comprehensive assessment and the current dietary standards of practice are then used to develop an individualized care plan to address the resident's specific nutritional concerns and preferences. The care plan must address, to the extent possible, identified causes of impaired nutritional status, reflect resident's goals and preferences, and identify interventions and the time frame and parameters for monitoring.

Regulatory Grouping for this F-tag is Quality of Care §483.25.

F800–Food and Nutrition Services

The facility must provide each resident with a nourishing, palatable, well-balanced diet that meets his or her daily nutritional and special dietary needs, taking into consideration the preferences of each resident.

Comments/Statements

CMS' guidance to surveyors on this issue is to ensure that facilities meet the requirement of having a system among all departments and disciplines that speak to the residents maintaining their daily nutritional status and dietary needs and choices. There must be ongoing communication and coordination among staffs of all departments to ensure that residents' assessments are completed accurately, that care plans are completed and carried out, and that the actual food served to the residents meets the residents' daily dietary needs and choices. Although there may be some challenges in meeting every resident's preferences, facilities must demonstrate that reasonable efforts are made to accommodate the choices and preferences of the residents.

Regulatory Grouping for this F-tag is Food and Nutrition Services §483.60.

F-801–Staffing

The facility must employ sufficient staff with the appropriate competencies and skills sets to carry out the functions of the food and nutrition service, taking into consideration resident assessments, individual plans of care and the number, acuity and diagnoses of the facility's resident population in accordance with the facility assessment required.

This includes a qualified dietitian or other clinically qualified nutrition professional either full-time, part-time, or on a consultant basis. A qualified dietitian or other clinically qualified nutrition professional is one who:

- **Holds a bachelor's or higher degree granted by a regionally accredited college or university in the United States (or equivalent foreign degree) with completion of the academic requirements of a program in nutrition or dietetics accredited by an appropriate national accreditation organization recognized for this purpose.**

- **Is licensed or certified as a dietitian or nutrition professional by the State in which the services are performed.**

- **Is recognized as a "registered dietitian" by the Commission on Dietetic Registration.**

- **For dietitians hired or contracted with prior to November 28, 2016, meets these requirements no later than 5 years after November 28, 2016, or as required by State law.**

If a qualified dietitian or other qualified nutrition professional is not employed full-time, the facility must designate a person to serve as the director of food and nutrition services who:

- **For designations prior to November 28, 2016, meets the following requirements no later than 5 years after November 28, 2016.**

    - **A certified dietary manager; or**

    - **A certified food service manager; or**

    - **Has similar national certification for food service management and safety from a national certifying body; or**

- **In States that have established standards for food service managers or dietary managers, meets State requirements for food service managers or dietary managers, and**

- **Receives frequently scheduled consultations from a qualified dietitian or other clinically qualified nutrition professional.**

Comments/Statements

CMS' guidance to surveyors for this F-Tag is for surveyors to ensure that the dietitian or clinically qualified nutrition professional, or food service director carry out the functions of the food and nutrition services to meet the needs of the residents. The functions at minimum should include:

- Assessing the nutritional needs of the residents.

- Developing and evaluating regular and therapeutic diets, including texture of the food, and liquids to meet residents' needs.

- Overseeing the budget and purchasing of food and supplies, and food preparation, service and storage.

- Participating in the QAPI when food and nutrition services are involved.

It is recommended that facilities follow their state requirements for credentials for their dietitians and food service management or supervisory staff.

Regulatory Grouping for this F-tag is Food and Nutrition Services §483.60.

F802–Staffing

The facility must employ sufficient staff with the appropriate competencies and skills sets to carry out the functions of the food and nutrition service, taking into consideration resident

assessments, individual plans of care and the number, acuity and diagnoses of the facility's resident population in accordance with the facility assessment required.

The facility must provide sufficient support personnel to safely and effectively carry out the functions of the food and nutrition service.

A member of the Food and Nutrition Services must participate on the interdisciplinary care plan team meetings.

Comments/Statements

Guidance to surveyors for this F-tag stresses the importance of observation by the surveyors. Surveyors will determine based on observations and interviews whether facility has sufficient support personnel to safely and effectively carry out the meal preparation, and other food and nutrition services as defined by facility's management. Also surveyors will observe whether meals intended to be served "hot" are served hot and are maintained at the desired temperature when provided to the residents. During interview surveyors will determine who represents food and nutrition service in the IDT meetings.

Regulatory Grouping for this F-tag is Food and Nutrition Services §483.60.

F803–Menus and nutritional adequacy

Menus must meet the nutritional needs of residents in accordance with established national guidelines. Menus must be prepared in advance and must be followed. Menus must reflect based on the facility's reasonable efforts, the religious, cultural and ethnic needs of the resident population, as well as input from residents and families. Menus must be updated periodically and reviewed by the facility's dietitian or other clinically qualified nutrition professional for nutritional adequacy.

Comments/Statements

Guidance to surveyors speaks to the need that facility not only provide food that is appetizing and culturally appropriate for the residents, but also addresses the alternatives aligned with individual needs and preferences if the primary menu does not meet the resident's liking.

Regulatory Grouping for this F-tag is Food and Nutrition services §483.60.

F804–Food and Drink

Each resident receives and the facility provides food prepared by methods that conserve nutritive value, flavor, and appearance. Food and drink that is palatable, and at a safe and appetizing temperature.

Comments/Statements

Facility must prepare food that will meet the satisfaction of the residents. Providing palatable, attractive (the food appearing good when served to residents), can help encourage the resident to increase their food intake, because this may also help prevent or aid in the recovery from injury or illness.

Facility must also ensure that food and drink are served at the required temperatures. Hot food is served hot and cold food served cold. The Food Service/Dietary Director or Manager must have the required temperatures for serving food. The log for food temperatures must be maintained by the cook, as surveyors check the log when they inspect the kitchen. Facilities must also get in the habit of doing periodic test trays to ensure that when the food is served to the residents, that the residents receive the food at the required temperatures.

Regulatory Grouping for this F-Tag is Food and Nutrition Services §483.60.

F805–Food and Drink

Each resident receives and the facility provides food in a form designed to meet the individual resident's needs.

Comments/Statements

The food must be prepared to meet residents needs according to the assessment and care plan of the residents. Residents with physician orders for cut, chopped, ground, or pureed meals must receive meals with that consistency.

Regulatory Grouping for this F-tag is Food and Nutrition Services §483.60.

F806–Food and Drink

Each resident receives and the facility provides food that accommodates allergies, intolerances, and preferences. Each resident must receive and the facility provides appealing options of

similar nutritive value to residents who choose not to eat food that is initially served, or who request a different meal choice.

Comments/Statements

It is the expectation that facilities must be aware of each resident's allergies, intolerances, and preferences and provide an appropriate alternate or substitute. If a resident refuses the meal served, resident should be given the opportunity to have a substitute. Food substitute should be consistent with the usual and/or ordinary food items provided by the facility. Does the facility have a system to communicate alternate food choices to the residents?

Regulatory Grouping for this F-tag is Food and Nutrition Services–§483.60.

F807–Food and Drink

Each resident receives and the facility provides drinks, including water and other liquids consistent with resident needs and preferences and sufficient to maintain resident hydration.

Comments/Statements

It is also highlighted in surveyor guidance that proper hydration alone is a critical aspect of nutrition among nursing home residents. It is noted also that individuals that do not receive adequate fluids are more susceptible to urinary tract infections, pneumonia, decubitus ulcers, skin infections, confusions, and disorientation.[8,9,10]

It is noted in this section that surveyors must review residents Comprehensive Assessments to determine whether resident's hydration status was assessed; also whether comprehensive care plan was developed to address resident's hydration and fluid needs.

Regulatory Grouping for this F-tag is Food and Nutrition Services §483.60

---

[8] Chidester, J.C. and Spangler, A.A."Fluid Intake in the Institutionalized Elderly", Journal of the American Dietetic Association 97 (1991): 23-30.

[9] Feinsod, F, Levenson, S, Rapp, M, Beechinor, E., Liebmann, L (2004) "Dehydration in frail, older residents in long term care facilities, "Journal of the American Medical Directors Association, 6(2 Suppl), s35-s41.

[10] Gasper, P.M. "Water Intake of Nursing Home Resident." Journal of Gerontologic Nursing. 1999; 25(4):22-29.

F808–Therapeutic Diets

Therapeutic diet must be prescribed by the attending physician. Effective November 28, 2017, the regulation defers to the State Regulation as to whether the attending physician may delegate to a registered nurse or a licensed dietitian the task of prescribing a resident's diet, including a therapeutic diet, to the extent allowed by the State law.

Comments/Statements

This part of the law is new, so administrators, Directors of Nursing, and Dietitian must check their State Law. If State law allows delegation of this task, and if the attending physician delegates this task, the attending physician must supervise the dietitian and must also be responsible for the resident's care.

It is also noted that the term "attending physician", or "physician" also includes non-physician provider such as physician assistant, nurse practitioner, or clinical nurse specialist.

Also addressed in this section is **"Mechanically altered diet"**–this diet is one in which the texture of the diet is altered. The type of texture must be specific and also must be prescribed by the attending physician, or delegated as allowed by State law.

Staff must recognize that if a resident has inadequate nutrition or nutritional deficits that may manifest into weight loss or other medical problems, the surveyor will check physician's order for proper diet order, including therapeutic diet or mechanically altered diet.

Regulatory Grouping for this F-tag is Food and Nutrition Services §483.60.

F809–Frequency of Meals

Each resident must receive and the facility must provide at least three meals daily, at regular times in comparable to meal times in the community, or in accordance with resident needs, preferences, requests, and plan of care.

There must be no more than 14 hours between a substantial evening meal and breakfast the following day; except when a nourishing snack is served at bedtime, up to 16 hours may elapse between a substantial evening meal and breakfast the following day if a resident group agrees to this meal span. Suitable, nourishing alternative meals and snacks must be provided to residents who want to eat at non-traditional times or outside of scheduled meal service times, consistent with the resident plan of care.

Comments/Statements

Nourishing snack is defined as items from the basic food groups. Suitable and nourishing alternate meals and snacks means that when the facility provides alternate meal or snack, the meal or snack is of similar nutritive value as the meal or snack offered at regular scheduled time which should be consistent with the resident's plan of care. Guidance to surveyor's state that it is not the intent of this regulation for facilities to provide a 24-hour-a-day full service food operation or an on-site chef.

Regulatory Grouping for this F-tag is Food and Nutrition Services §483.60.

F810–Assistive Devices

The facility must provide special eating equipment and utensils for residents who need them, and appropriate assistance to ensure that the resident can use the assistive devices when consuming meals and snacks.

Comments/Statements

The concern is that residents, who have the capacity and capability to eat independently with assistive devices, based on their comprehensive assessments and plan of care, that these residents must be provided with special eating adaptive devices, and encouraged by staff to eat independently with these devices. Is facility monitoring residents to see if staff is assisting residents, and if residents are using these assistive devices if the resident(s) will benefit from this?

Regulatory Grouping for this F-tag is Food and Nutrition Services §483.60.

F811–Paid Feeding Assistants

State approved training course. A facility may use a paid feeding assistant, if the feeding assistant successfully completed a State-approved training course that meets the requirements, and the feeding assistants program is consistent with the State law.

A feeding assistant must work under the supervision of a registered nurse (RN) or a licensed practical nurse (LPN). In an emergency, a feeding assistant must call a supervisory nurse for help. For resident selection criteria, the facility must ensure that the feeding assistant provides dining assistance only for residents who have no complicated feeding problems, such as difficulty swallowing, recurrent lung aspiration, and tube or parenteral/IV feedings.

The facility must base resident selection on the interdisciplinary team's assessment and the resident's latest assessment and plan of care.

Comments/Statements

Feeding assistants training must be State –approved training course for feeding assistants. The facility must maintain a record of all individuals, used by the facility as feeding assistants, and these individuals must have completed the State-approved training courses. The Interdisciplinary Team must make a determination based on the resident's comprehensive assessment in order to determine whether the resident will benefit from a paid feeding assistant, and this must be care planned and documented by the IDT team. Paid feeding assistants are only allowed to assist residents who do not have any complicated eating or drinking problems of fluids.

Facilities must verify that employees hired as paid feeding assistant have completed the State-approved training. Facilities who use temporary agencies must also verify that paid feeding assistants have completed the State-approved training courses. When surveyors conduct their surveys and a facility has paid feeding assistants, the surveyors will review the facility's records to ensure that the facility has the proper required documents for the paid feeding assistants program.

Regulatory Grouping for this F-tag is Food and Nutrition Services §483.60.

F812–Food Safety Requirements

The Facility must procure food from sources approved or considered satisfactory by federal and state authorities. Facility must store, prepare, distribute and serve food in accordance with professional standards for food service safety.

Regulation defines "professional standards for food safety" to mean sanitary conditions and the prevention of foodborne illness. Foodborne illness refers to illness caused by the ingestion of contaminated food or beverages.

Comments/Statements

This section of the F-tag gives an overview on the importance of safe food handling. It is noted that nursing home residents risk of serious complications from foodborne illness as a result of their compromised health status. Unsafe food handling practices represent a potential source of pathogen exposure for residents. Sanitary conditions must be present in health care food service settings to promote safe food handling. For food handling, CMS recognizes that U.S. Food and Drug Administration's (FDA) Food Code and the Centers for Disease Control and Prevention's (CDC) food safety guidance as national standards to procure, store, prepare, distribute, and serve food for long term care facilities in a safe and sanitary manner. Operational steps that are identified that are critical to control in facilities to prevent or eliminate food safety hazards are: thawing, cooking, cooling, holding, reheating of foods, and employee hygiene practices.

Facilities are directed to additional websites regarding safe food handling to minimize the potential for foodborne illness:

National Food Safety Information Network's Gateway to Government Food Safety Information at http://www.FoodSafety.gov.

U.S. Food & Drug Administration Food Code Web site at http://www.fda.gov/Food/GuidanceRegulation/RetailFoodProtection/FoodCode/.

Employee Health falls under this category for Infection Control purposes. Important Infection Control factors include:

- Guidance to surveyors that stress those employees who handle food must be free from communicable diseases and infected skin lesions. The regulation also mandates that facilities must have an infection prevention and infection control program. The infection control program must also include policies and procedures that address circumstances that prohibit employees from direct contact with residents or their food.

- Hand Washing, Gloves, and Antimicrobial Gel–Employees should never use bare hands to handle food ready or otherwise.

- Disposable gloves must be used and employees must wash hands before putting on gloves and after removing gloves. Disposable gloves must be discarded after use. Disposable gloves are considered single use items.

- Employees must consistently practice good hand hygiene.

- Dietary/Food Service employees must wear hairnet, hat or beard restraint.

- Staff should maintain nails that are clean and neat, and to keep jewelry at a minimum, and wear intact disposable gloves in good condition that are changed appropriately to reduce spread of infection.

- Appropriate hand hygiene must be practiced between residents after direct contact with residents' skin or secretions.

Employee Health: Infection Control requires a facility to have an infection prevention and control program that specifies policies for, among other things, the circumstances under which a facility must prohibit an employee from direct contact with residents or their food.
—**Reference F880 §483.80**

Regulatory Grouping for this F-tag is Food and Nutrition Services §483.60.

F880–Infection Control

The facility must establish and maintain an infection prevention and control program designed to provide a safe, sanitary and comfortable environment and to help prevent the development and transmission of communicable diseases and infection. The facility must establish an infection prevention and control program (IPCP) that must include, at minimum, the following elements:

- A system for preventing, identifying, reporting, investigating, and controlling infections and communicable diseases for all residents, staff, volunteers, visitors, and other individuals providing services for the facility.

- Written standards, policies, and procedures for the program which must include:

    - A system of surveillance designed to identify communicable disease.

    - When and to whom possible incidents of communicable disease or infection should be reported.

    - Standard and transmission-based precautions to be followed.

    - When and how isolation should be used for residents.

    - The circumstances under which facility must prohibit employees with a communicable disease or infected skin lesions from direct contact with residents or their food, if direct contact will transmit the disease.

    - The hand hygiene procedures to be followed by staff involved in direct resident contact.

- A system for recording incidents identified under the facility's IPCP and corrective actions taken.

- Linens–personnel must handle, store, process, and transport linens to prevent spread of infection.

- Annual reviews–facility must conduct annual review of its IPCP and update the program as necessary.

Below are definitions for terminology as outlined in Regulations:

- "Airborne precautions"–actions taken to prevent or minimize the transmission of infectious agents/organisms that remain infectious over long distance when suspended in the air.

- "Alcohol-based hand rub (ABHR)"–a 60-95 percent ethanol or isopropyl alcohol-containing preparation base designed for application to the hands to reduce the number of viable microorganisms.

- "Cleaning"–removal of visible soil from objects and surfaces using water or detergents or enzymatic products.

- "Cohorting"–the practice of grouping residents infected or colonized with the same infectious agent together to confine their care to one area and prevent contact with susceptible residents.

- "Colonization"–the presence of microorganisms on or within body sites without detectable host immune response, cellular damage, or clinical expression.

- "Communicable disease"–an infection transmissible by direct contact with an affected individual or the individual's body fluids or by indirect means.

- "Community-acquired infections"–infections that are present or incubating at the time of admission and which generally develop within 72 hours of admission.

- "Contact precaution"–measures that are intended to prevent transmission of infectious agents which are spread by direct or indirect contact with the resident or the resident's environment.

- "Droplet precautions"–actions designed to reduce/prevent the transmission of pathogens spread through close respiratory or mucous membrane contact with secretions.

- "Hand hygiene"–a general term that applies to hand washing, antiseptic hand wash, and alcohol-based hand rub.

- "Infection"–the establishment of an infective agent in or a suitable host, producing clinical signs and symptoms (e.g. fever, redness, heat, purulent, etc.).

- "Infection Preventionist" term used for the person(s) designated by the facility to be responsible for the infection prevention and control program.

- "Isolation Precaution"–actions (precautions) implemented, in addition to standard precautions, that are based upon the means of transmission (airborne, contact, droplet) in order to prevent or control infections.

- "Personal Protective Equipment (PPE)"–protective items or garments worn to protect the body or clothing from hazards that can cause injury and to protect residents from cross-contamination.

- "Standard Precautions"–infection prevention practices that apply to all residents, regardless of suspected or confirmed diagnosis or presumed infection status. Standard precautions are based on the principle that all blood, body fluids, secretions, excretions except sweat, regardless of whether they contain visible blood, non-intact skin, and mucous membranes may contain transmissible infectious agents.

- "Transmission-based Precautions"–Also known as "Isolation Precautions", these are actions implemented, in addition to standard precautions, that are based upon the means of transmission (whether airborne, contact, and droplet) in order to prevent or control infections.

Expectation of CMS for Facilities' Infection Prevention and Control Program:
CMS expects facilities to:

- Establish and maintain an IPCP designed to provide a safe, sanitary, and comfortable environment and to help prevent the development and transmission of communicable diseases and infection.

- Utilize a IPCP program that follows national standards and guidelines.

- Tailor the emphasis of their IPCP for visitors too.

- Work to prevent transmission of infection to the resident from the visitor using reasonable precautions and national standards.

- Also utilize passive screening such as signs at the entrance or lobby of the facility to alert visitors with signs and symptoms of communicable diseases not to enter the facility.

- Ensure visitor follow facility's policies for prevention of transmission (e.g. follow respiratory hygiene/cough etiquette procedures) if the visitor must enter the facility.

- Ensure that the system include the following parts or components.

- A system for preventing, identifying, reporting, investigating, and controlling infections and communicable diseases that covers residents, staff, volunteers, visitors, and others, that is based on the facilities assessment and that follows national standards.

- Policies and procedures–facility must have written policies and procedures in accordance with the regulation. Policies & Procedures must:

  - Policy must be reviewed at minimum annually and revised based on facility assessment.

  - Have ongoing system of surveillance.

  - Have information as to when and to whom possible incident of communicable diseases must be reported to within the facility.

  - Have information as to which communicable disease must be reported to local/state public health authorities.

  - Have information as to how to use standard precautions and how and when to use transmission-based precautions.

  - Have information as to the selection and use of PPE (personal protective equipment).

  - Address the provision of facemasks for residents with new respiratory symptoms.

  - The process to manage a resident on a transmission-based precaution when a single/private room is not available.

  - Limiting the movement of a resident with highly infectious diseases.

  - Respiratory Hygiene/Cough Etiquette.

- A system for recording incidents identified under the IPCP and corrective actions taken by the facility.

- An antibiotic stewardship program.

- Written Occupational/Employee Health Policies that address:

  - Reporting of staff illness and following work restrictions based on national standards and guidelines.

- Prohibiting contact with residents or their food when staff have potentially communicable disease or infected skin lesions.

- Assessing risk for tuberculosis (TB).

- Monitoring for clusters or outbreaks of illness among staff.

- Implementing exposure control plan.

- Education and competency assessment: facility must ensure staff follow the IPCP's standards, policies, and procedures.

Infection Prevention and Control has been revised by CMS with the expectation as stated above, that facilities establish and maintain an IPCP designed to provide a safe, sanitary, and comfortable environment and to help prevent the development and transmission of communicable diseases and infections. The program must have a system to prevent, identify, report, investigate, and control infections and communicable diseases for all residents, staff, and visitors. The revised Infection Prevention and Control regulation is very extensive, and has an additional new requirement that the facility must have an Infection Preventionist in the facility.

It should be noted here that there are additional upcoming requirements for the new infection preventions; the detailed training for this individual, qualifications, and hourly requirements for this individual does not come into effect until implementation of Phase 3.

CMS has also implemented Facility Assessment protocol for facilities to determine what resources are needed by the facilities to care for their residents competently during both day-to-day operations and during emergencies. It is also CMS' expectation for facilities to conduct a facility-wide assessment and document this data on an ongoing basis. Facilities must also conduct an annual review of their facility assessments and update the document as required.

Regulatory Grouping for this F-tag is Infection Control §483.80.

F920–Requirements for Dining and Resident Activities

The facility must provide appropriate one or more rooms designated for resident dining and activities. The room must be well lighted, well ventilated, adequately furnished and must have sufficient space to accommodate all activities.

The furnishings must be structurally sound; there must be chairs of varying sizes to accommodate residents varying needs of residents. Wheelchairs must be able to fit under the dining room tables.

Comments/Statements

The room must be large enough and have flexibility for staff to arrange furniture to accommodate residents who use wheelchairs, walkers, and other mobility aids.

Regulatory Grouping for this F-tag is Physical Environment §483.90.

F947–Required In-Service Training for Nurse Aides

In-service training must be sufficient to ensure the continuing competence of nurse aides, but must be no less than 12 hours per year. The training must include dementia management training and resident abuse prevention training.

The training must also include areas that have been assessed as weakness in the nurse aides' performance reviews and facility assessments. The training may also address the special needs of the residents as determined by the facility staff. For those nurse aides that provide services and care for individuals with cognitive impairments, the training must also address the care of the cognitively impaired.

Comments/Statements

CMS has placed great emphasis on staff competencies so it is important that Staff Development Director also ensure that all staffs, nursing at all level, Food Service staff, and all disciplines and departments receive the required training upon initial orientation and periodic routine training based on frequency established by the facility.

The guidance to surveyors also making recommendations those facilities can use a variety of training methods that could be facilitated through any combination of in-person instruction, webinars, and /or supervised practical training hours. Surveyors may review the training log of the facility to determine attendance by the nurse aides at the training. When surveyors observe nurse aides working with, interacting with, or providing care and service for residents, they (surveyors) could make a determination whether the nurse aide(s) need training based on the manner in which the nurse does his/her work.

Regulatory Grouping for this F-tag is Training Requirements §483.95.

F948–Required training of Feeding Assistants

A facility must not use any individual working in the facility as a paid feeding assistant unless that individual has successfully completed a State-approved training program for feeding

assistants. **A facility must maintain a record of all individuals, used by the facility as feeding assistants, who have successfully completed the training course for paid feeding assistants.**

A state-approved training course for paid feeding assistants must include, at minimum, 8 hours of training in the following:

- Feeding techniques.

- Assistance with feeding and hydration.

- Communication and interpersonal skills.

- Appropriate responses to resident behavior.

- Safety and emergency procedures, including the Heimlich maneuver.

- Infection control.

- Resident rights.

- Recognizing changes in residents that are inconsistent with their normal behavior and the importance of reporting those.

CMS has expectation that facilities will follow the State approved requirements for Feeding Assistants. If surveyors have concern about the paid feeding assistants, they will demand proof that the paid feeding assistants have documented evidence that they completed the State-approved training.

Regulatory Grouping for this F-tag is Training Requirements §483.95.

RESIDENT MEAL TIME AND DINING EXPERIENCE MONITORING TOOL

Observation during Meal Time

F550–Resident's Dignity and Self Respect

Regulation & Interpretive Guidelines	Compliance Y / N / NA	Comments
Is the resident well groomed?		
Is the resident encouraged and assisted to dress in his/her own clothes to the dining room?		
Does staff make residents' meals available to all residents at the table as soon as meal is delivered to the unit/floor dining room?		
Does staff provide napkins and non-disposable cutlery and flatware to eat their meal?		
Does staff sit beside the resident while feeding the resident as opposed to standing?		
Does staff interact and speak to the resident while assisting that resident with meal as oppose carrying social conversation across the room with other staff while feeding the resident?		
Does staff address resident in respectful and courteous manner?		

	Compliance Y/N/NA	Comments
Does staff allow resident to eat their meal at their own pace as opposed to rushing resident to finish meal?		
Does staff maintain a quiet dining room experience with little or no loud talking amongst staff members?		
Does the staff respond to resident's request in a timely manner?		
If resident requires medication prior to meal time does the staff/nurse ensure the resident receive the medication as ordered?		

F584–Homelike Environment

Regulation & Interpretive Guidelines	Compliance Y / N / NA	Comments
If the resident refuses to go to the dining room, does the staff allow the resident to eat where he or she wants to eat, lounge, or in resident's room?		
Does the staff allow the resident to eat when he/she wants to eat?		
Does the staff serve the residents' meal in a homelike manner in the dining room as oppose to serving the meal on trays?		
Does the staff allow the resident to have their preferences or substitutes?		
When the resident requests a substitute does the resident receive the substitute in a reasonable timeframe?		

Does the facility have proper system to help residents' food preferences communicated to the food service/dietary department?		
Does the facility routinely provide comfortable temperature levels for residents?		
Does the facility provide temperature that is maintained between 71-81 degrees Fahrenheit range for good dining experience for residents?		
Does the facility maintain comfortable sound levels for the residents?		
Is there background noise in the facility while residents are eating their meals?		
Do the dining room tables allow adequate space and height for residents in wheelchairs to sit comfortably for their meals?		
Are the dining room chairs structurally in good condition?		

NOTES

F635–Admission Orders

Regulation & Interpretive Guidelines	Compliance Y / N / NA	Comments
Does the resident have doctor's orders for his/her diet?		
Is the resident receiving the proper diet ordered by his/her doctor?		
If therapeutic diet is ordered does the resident receive therapeutic diet?		

F675 Quality of Life, F676–A resident's abilities in activities of daily living relative to eating

Regulation & Interpretive Guidelines	Compliance Y / N / NA	Comments
Is the staff aware that the regulation states that the resident's abilities in activities of daily living (ADL) do not diminish unless circumstances of the individual clinical condition demonstrate that diminution was unavoidable?		
For resident requiring assistance, does the staff give resident the required assistance as stated in care plan?		
Does the resident need assistive device/utensils to eat meal?		
If yes, is the assistive device(s) provided for the resident to eat independently if preferred by resident?		
Does the resident need cueing or prompting to eat and are staffs providing the required assistance?		
For residents requiring feeding, are residents being fed timely when the food is delivered?		
Is food served to resident within the required food temperature for both hot and cold food items?		

Are all nursing staffs available to assist during meal time to ensure all residents receive their meal timely?		
Are staffs aware of risk factors that may affect the resident's eating abilities to chew and swallow?		
Are the staffs aware of the residents' allergies, intolerances, and preferences?		
Are staffs aware of person-centered care, and the need to support residents to making their choices?		
How well does the staff know the wishes of the resident–does the staff know whether the resident likes to eat in his/her room or in the dining room?		
Does the staff know the resident's food likes and dislikes?		
Does the staff know whether the resident prefers to eat at different times as opposed to the scheduled meal times?		

F677–Requirement for facility to ensure that a resident who is unable to carry out activities of daily living receives the necessary services to maintain good nutrition, grooming, and personal and oral hygiene

Regulation & Interpretive Guidelines	Compliance Y / N / NA	Comments
Are the staffs fully aware of the level of assistance needed by the resident?		
Do the staffs demonstrate their awareness to provide the necessary services for the residents to maintain good nutrition, grooming, and oral hygiene, for those residents who cannot carry out activities of daily living for themselves?		
Is the staff aware of the services for oral hygiene include brushing the teeth, cleaning dentures, cleaning the mouth and tongue either by assisting the resident with a mouth wash or by manual cleaning with gauze sponge?		

NOTES

F804–Food and Drink–the resident must receive and the facility must provide food that conserve nutritive value, flavor, and appearance; and that the food is palatable, attractive and served at the proper temperature

Regulation & Interpretive Guidelines	Compliance Y / N / NA	Comments
For resident who may require mechanical soft or puree diet, does the food look attractive on the plate?, does the food service/dietitian know whether the food is palatable, and does the food preserve the nutritive value?		
Does facility serve the resident food at the required food temperature?		
Do the residents' meals routinely look attractive on the plate, and palatable?		
Do residents express satisfaction with meal served?		

F807–Substitutes–Food prepared and offered as substitutes of similar nutritive value to residents who refuse food served

When a resident refuses the food served, is the resident offered a substitute of similar nutritive value?		
Is the substitute consistent with the usual food items provided by the facility?		
Do the staffs anticipate substitutes based on the resident's food likes and dislikes compared to the menu items?		
Do the residents have to wait long periods for the substitute to be delivered to them?		
Does the substitute have similar nutritive value as the original menu item?		

F806–Therapeutic Diets

Is the resident receiving therapeutic diet?		
Is resident receiving the right therapeutic diet prescribed by the resident's attending physician?		
Do the kitchen staffs accurately identify the residents that need therapeutic diets?		

F809–Frequency of Meals/Snacks at Bedtime

Regulation & Interpretive Guidelines	Compliance Y / N / NA	Comments
Does the facility provide at least three meals a day at regular intervals as comparable to that in the community for the residents?		
Is the interval between substantial evening meal and breakfast the following day about 14 hours or less?		
Does the facility offer snacks at bedtime daily?		
When snacks are routinely offered at bedtime, does the facility offer breakfast a little beyond 14 hours but not to exceed 16 hours between the substantial evening meal and breakfast the following day?		

F811–Paid Feeding Assistants

Does the facility have paid feeding assistants on staff?		
If answer is yes, does the facility limit paid feeding assistants services only to residents who do not have complicated feeding problems?		

Are the paid feeding assistants supervised by RNs or LPNs?		
Are paid feeding assistants utilized according to your State law?		

F920–Dining and Resident Activities Rooms

Is the designated dining room well ventilated, with good air circulation?		
Is the dining room adequately furnished?		
Are chairs of appropriate and varying sizes meet the varying needs of the residents?		
Can wheelchairs fit comfortably under the dining room table?		
Is there sufficient space to accommodate all residents that want to eat in the dining room?		

F947–Required In-Service Training for Nurse Aides

Regulation & Interpretive Guidelines	Compliance Y / N / NA	Comments
As direct care givers, do nurse aides demonstrate their proficiency and skills in taking care of the residents' special needs as identified in resident assessments, and care plan?		
Is the staff providing the activities of daily living services to meet the needs of the residents?		
In addition to meeting the feeding needs of the residents, do the nurse aides provide adequate liquid to meet residents' needs?		

Do the nurse aides have training in dementia management to meet the needs of residents with dementia?		
Do the nurse aides have training in prevention of abuse?		

F948–Training for Feeding Assistants

Regulation & Interpretive Guidelines	Compliance Y / N / NA	Comments
Have the feeding assistants successfully completed a State-approved training program?		
Did the feeding assistant(s) take the courses in Feeding techniques, Assistance with feeding and hydration?		
Did the feeding assistant(s) take the courses in Resident Rights, Communication and interpersonal skills, Appropriate responses to resident behavior?		
Did the feeding assistants take the course in Safety and emergency procedures including the Heimlich maneuver, Recognizing changes in resident that are inconsistent with their normal behavior, Infection control.		

NOTES

REGULATION F-TAGS
FOR KITCHEN AND FOOD SERVICE

Regulation: 42 CFR §483.60(i)(1)(2): Food Procurement, Store/Prepare/Serve–Sanitary

§483.60(i)(4): Dispose Garbage & Refuse Properly;

§483.80(a)(1)(2)(4)(e)(f): Infection Prevention & Control;

§483.90(d)(2): Essential Equipment, Safe Operating Condition

§483.90(i)(4): Maintains Effective Pest Control Program

BELOW ARE THE NEW F-TAGS, FEDERAL REGULATIONS, portions/sections of the guidance to surveyors and comments from the author relative to Kitchen and Food Service operations. These have been arranged in an easy to read, easy to follow, and abridged format, with the important parts for faster reading and quick reference for staff. The author has taken every effort to include salient portions of the regulations, guidance to surveyors, and her comments to reinforce important points. It is also advisable for staffs to secure additional resources, including Federal and State Regulations.

F-TAGS FOR KITCHEN AND FOOD SERVICE

F804–Food and Drink

EACH RESIDENT RECEIVES AND THE FACILITY PROVIDES **food prepared by methods that conserve nutritive value, flavor, and appearance. Food and drink that is palatable, and at a safe and appetizing temperature.**

Also see F804 in Part II page 61.

F812–Food Safety Requirements

The facility must procure food from sources approved or considered satisfactory by federal, state, or local authorities. The facility must store, prepare, distribute and serve food in accordance with professional standards for food service safety.

Also see F812 on Part II page 65 for definitions for "professional standards for food safety" and for "Foodborne illness". Also see section on Infection Control factors.

Food Storage in the Food Service Department/Kitchen:

- Dry Food Storage–Dry storage may be in a room or area designed for the storage of dry goods, such as single service items, canned goods, and packaged or containerized bulk food that is not Potentially Hazardous Foods (PHF)/ or Time/Temperature Control for Safety (TCS). The main focus for dry storage is to keep un-refrigerated foods, disposable dishware, and napkins in a clean, dry area, which is free from contaminants. Dry foods and goods must be stored in a manner to keep their integrity of the packaging until they are ready to use. It is the recommendation that food such as flour or sugar that are stored in bins, be removed from their original packaging. Food and food products must always be kept off the floor and clear off the ceiling.

- **Refrigerated Storage**–PHF/TCS foods must be maintained at or below 41 degrees F, unless otherwise specified by law. Refrigeration prevents food from becoming a hazard by significantly slowing the growth of most microorganisms. Foods in walk-in unit should be stored off the floor.

- Frozen foods must be maintained at a temperature to keep the food frozen solid.

Practices to maintain safe refrigerated storage include:

- Monitor food temperatures and functioning of the refrigeration equipment daily and at routine intervals during all hours of operation. Most facilities maintain a refrigeration log where staff records the temperatures at certain interval daily.

- Placing hot food in shallow pans to permit food to cool rapidly.

- Separating raw foods (e.g. beef, fish, pork, poultry) from each other and storing raw meat on shelves below fruits, vegetables, or ready-to-eat foods so meat juices do not drip onto these foods.

- Labeling, dating, and monitoring refrigerated foods including leftovers, so the food is used by the use-by-date.

Safe Food Preparation

- Thawing–some food may not be thawed at room temperature, because they may reach their danger zone for rapid bacteria proliferation.

- Thaw food in the refrigerator and manner that prevents cross-contamination.

- Thaw food by completely submerge the food under cold water.

- Thawing as part of the continuous cooking process.

Final Cooking Temperatures

Monitoring the food's internal temperature is important and will help ensure microorganisms can no longer survive and food is safe for consumption. Foods listed below should reach the following internal temperatures:

- Poultry and stuffed foods (turkey, pork chop, chicken, etc.) 165 degrees F.

- Ground meat (ground beef, ground pork), ground fish, and eggs at least 155 degrees F.

- Fish and other non-ground meat 145 degrees F.

- If the facility is using unpasteurized eggs, these eggs must be cooked until parts of the egg are completely firm, regardless of the resident's request for such things as "sunny side up".

Reheating Foods

- Reheated cooked foods present a risk because they have passed through the danger zone multiple times during cooking, cooling, and reheating.

- The PHF/TCS food that is cooked and cooled must be reheated so that all parts of the food reach an internal temperature of 165 degrees F for at least 15 seconds before holding for hot service.

Cooling

- Improper cooling is a major factor in causing foodborne illness.

- Taking too long to chill PHF/TCS foods has been consistently identified as one factor contributing to foodborne illness.

- Large or dense food items, such as roasts, turkeys, soups, stews, legumes, and chili may require interventions (e.g. placing foods in shallow pans, cutting roasts into smaller portions, utilizing ice water baths, and stirring periodically) in order to be chilled safely within an allowed time period. These foods take a long time to cool because of their volume and density.

- Cooked potentially hazardous foods that are subject to time and temperature control for safety are best cooled rapidly within 2 hours, from 135 to 70 degrees F and within 4 more hours to the temperature of approximately 41 degrees F.

Modified Consistency

- Residents who require a modified consistency diet may be at risk for developing foodborne illness because of the increased number of food handling steps required when preparing pureed and other modified consistency foods.

- When hot pureed, ground, or diced food drop into the danger zone (below 135 degrees F), the mechanically altered food must be reheated to 165 degrees F for 15 seconds if holding for hot service.

Eggs

- Pooled eggs are raw eggs that have been cracked and combined together.

- Facility should only crack enough eggs for immediate service to a resident's request.

- Unpasteurized eggs–Salmonella infections may be prevented by substituting unpasteurized eggs with pasteurized eggs in preparation of foods that will not be thoroughly cooked, such as Caesar dressing, etc.

- Raw eggs with damaged shells are also unsafe because of the potential for contamination.

Food Service and Distribution

- The various systems available for serving and distributing food items to residents include:
    - Tray lines.
    - Portable steam tables transported to the unit or dining area.
    - Open shelved food transport cart with covered trays.
    - Enclosed carts that have hot and cold compartment.

- The purpose of these systems is to provide safe holding and transport of the food to the resident's location.

- Food safety requires consistent temperature control from the tray line to transport and distribution to prevent contamination.

- The tray line may include, but is not limited to the steam table where hot prepared foods are held and served, and the chilled are where cold foods are held and served. While PHF/TCS foods are on the tray line, the temperature of the foods should be periodically monitored throughout the meal service to ensure proper hot or cold holding temperatures are maintained.

- **Food Distribution**–Food may be distributed to different locations where residents eat their meal. These can be in the dining rooms in different floors, it can be at residents' rooms. Staffs need to be cautious of potential food handling problems such as:

  - Staff distributing trays without first properly washing their hands.

  - Serving food to residents after collecting soiled plates and food waste, without properly washing their hands.

- **Snacks**

  - Snacks refer to food served between meals or at bed time.

  - Temperature control and freedom from contamination are also important when ready-to-eat or prepared food items for snacks are sent to the unit and are held for delivery, stored at the nursing station, or the unit refrigerator, nursing cupboard, or stored in the resident's personal refrigerator in resident's room.

- **Transported Foods**

  - If a resident takes prepared foods with him/her out of the facility (e.g. bag lunch to dialysis, clinics, sporting events, or day treatment program) the food must be handled and prepared for the resident with the same safe and sanitary approaches used during primary food preparation in the facility.

- **Ice**

  - Appropriate ice and water handling practices prevent contamination and the potential for waterborne illness.

  - Ice must be made from potable water.

  - Ice that is used to cool food items (e.g. ice in a pan used to cool milk cartons) is not to be used for consumption.

  - Keeping the ice machine clean and sanitary will help prevent contamination of the ice.

  - Staff, residents, visitors, etc. must wash hands adequately, and use the scoop to handle the ice in the ice machine.

- Staff, residents, visitors, etc. must not use their bare hands to handle ice.

- Ice chests or coolers used to store and transport ice should be cleaned regularly.

- **Refrigeration**

  - The facility refrigerator must be in good working condition to keep food at or below 41 degrees F or less.

  - The freezer must be in good working condition and the freezer must keep frozen food solid.

  - Document the temperature of external and internal refrigerator gauges as well as the temperature inside the refrigerator. Measure whether the temperature of a PHF/TCS food is 41 degrees or less. Keep a log of the daily readings monthly outside the refrigerator door of the temperatures, and place the log in a binder at the end of the month.

  - Check the firmness of frozen food and inspect the wrapper to determine if it is intact enough to protect the food.

  - Food service Director/Manager/Supervisor should check with their staff periodically to see if they are checking the log daily to make sure the refrigerator and freezer are working properly.

  - Food Service Director/Manager/Supervisor should ask the food service workers if they know the procedure for reporting if the refrigerator or freezer is not working properly.

  - Unit Refrigerators

    - Temperature control and freedom from contamination is also important when food and snacks are sent to the unit and held at the unit nursing station, held in the cupboard, or placed in the unit refrigeration.

    - Food must not be left on trays or countertops beyond safe time and/or beyond safe temperature.

    - Food must not be left in the unit refrigerator beyond safe "use by" dates; this also includes food that were opened but not labeled.

- **Machine Washing and Sanitizing**: Below are general recommendations according to the U.S. Department of Health and Human Services, Public Health Services, Food and Drug Administration Food Code for each method.

  - High Temperature Dishwasher (heat sanitization):
    - Wash–150-165 degrees F.
    - Final Rinse–180 degrees F.
  - Low Temperature Dishwasher (chemical sanitization):
    - Wash–120 degrees F.
    - Final Rinse–50 ppm (parts per million) hypochlorite (chlorine) on dish surface in final rinse.
    - The chemical solution must be maintained at the correct concentration, based on periodic testing at least once per shift.

- **Manual Washing and Sanitizing**
  - A 3-step process is used to manually wash, rinse, and sanitize dishware correctly.
  - The first step is thorough washing using hot water and detergent.
  - The second step is rinsing with hot water to remove all soap residues.
  - The third step is sanitizing with hot water or chemical solution maintained at the correct concentration.
  - Facilities must have adequate and appropriate testing equipment, such as test strips and thermometer to ensure adequate washing and sufficient concentration of sanitizing solution is present.
  - Food preparation equipment and utensils must be air dried.

- Cleaning Fixed Equipment
  - When cleaning fixed equipment (e.g. mixers, slicers, etc.) the removable parts must be washed and sanitized.

- The non-removable parts must be cleaned with detergent and hot water, rinsed, air-dried and sprayed with sanitizing solution.

- Finally, the equipment is reassembled.

Regulatory Grouping for this F-tag is Food and Nutrition Services §483.60.

F813–Food Safety Requirements

The facility must have a policy regarding use and storage of foods brought to residents by family and other visitors to ensure safe and sanitary storage, handling, and consumption. The policy must include ensuring that facility staff assists the resident in accessing and consuming the food, if the resident is not able to do so on his or her own. Facility also has the responsibility to help families and visitors understand safe food handling.

Comments/Statements

This is an important new F-Tag and it is CMS' expectation that facilities develop policies and procedures to address food brought from the outside for residents, by families and visitors.

Regulatory Grouping for this F-tag is Food and Nutrition Services §483.60.

F814–Food Safety Requirements: Garbage and Refuse Disposal Properly

The facility must dispose of garbage and refuse properly.

Comments/Statements

Surveyors check and observe all areas inside and outside of the kitchen. They observe:

- Whether garbage and refuse containers are in good condition with no leaks.

- Whether waste is placed in dumpsters or compactors and the lids are covered.

- Whether loading docks are used to store garbage and refuse.

- Whether garbage receptacles are covered when removed from kitchen area to dumpster.

- Whether food carts and clean food transport are kept clean with no odors or waste fat.

Regulatory Grouping for this F-tag is Food and Nutrition Services §483.60.

F880–Infection Control

See Infection Control in the Part II on page 67.

F908–Maintain all Mechanical, Electrical, and Patient Care Equipment in safe Operating Condition.

- **Facility must ensure that all mechanical, electrical, and patient care equipment is maintained in safe operating condition.**

Comments/Statements

When surveyors walk in the kitchen to inspect during survey process, they inspect the following equipment to make sure they are in safe working/operating condition, according to manufactures' recommendations. The surveyors will inspect:

- Kitchen walk-in refrigerator(s)
- Freezer
- Dish Washing machine
- Food slicers
- Food Mixer(s)
- Ovens
- Nursing Unit refrigerators
- Resident personal refrigerator(s)
- Etc.

Regulatory Grouping for this F-tag is Physical Environment §483.90.

F925–Maintain an Effective Pest Control Program

- **The facility must maintain an effective pest control program so that the facility is free of pest and rodents.**

Comments/Statements

CMS defines "effective pest control program" as measures to eradicate and contain common household pests (e.g. roaches, ants, mosquitoes, flies, mice, rats and lice and bed bugs).

Kitchen/Food Service staff, administrator, Director of Nursing and Quality Assurance Performance Improvement Director/Coordinator need to make sure that there are no pest control issues in the kitchen. They must ensure that the facility has a solid pest control program with an effective pest control vendor that does regular routine treatment of the facility. There should be no roaches, flies, ants, mice, or rats, in or around the kitchen area. If the surveyor(s) see evidence of pest infestation in a particular space, this is a very serious issue that may border on very serious deficiency or deficiencies.

Regulatory Grouping for this F-tag is Physical Environment §483.90.

KITCHEN AND FOOD SERVICE MONITORING TOOL

F804–Food

Regulation & Interpretive Guideline	Compliance Y / N / NA	Comments
Does the facility prepare food by methods to conserve the flavor, appearance and nutritive value of the food?		
Is the food palatable, attractive and prepared at the proper temperature?		

F812–Food Procurement: Store/Prepare/Serve–Sanitary

Regulation & Interpretive Guideline	Compliance Y / N / NA	Comments
Does the facility procure food from approved and satisfactory sources?		
Is food stored properly under sanitary conditions?		
Is raw meat stored away from vegetable and other foods in the refrigerator?		
Is raw meat stored separately from cooked foods when stored in the refrigerator?		
Is staff aware of the required temperatures that foods must be cooked, maintained and stored in order to prevent food borne illness?		
Is staff aware that hot foods should leave the kitchen or steam table above 140° F		

Is staff aware that cold food should leave the kitchen at or below 41° F?		
Is staff aware that freezer temperatures should be 0° F or below and food should be frozen solid when in the freezer?		
Is staff aware that refrigerator temperature should be maintained at 41° F or Below?		
Does the staff label and date leftover food stored in the refrigerator?		
Does the staff wash their hands prior to preparing, serving and distributing food?		
Is frozen food thawed in the refrigerator?		
Does the staff use sanitized thermometer to evaluate food temperatures?		
Are potentially hazardous foods kept at an internal temperature of 41° F or below in cold food storage unit, or at internal temperature of 140° F or above in hot food storage unit during display and service?		
Is leftover food heated to the appropriate temperatures?		
Does staff minimize hand contact with food?		
Does the food delivery system to residents' dining room and resident rooms protect the food from contamination?		
Are hand-washing facilities convenient and properly equipped for dietary staff and dietary service use?		
Are cans and containers of food stored properly off the floor and on clean surfaces to prevent contamination in dry food storage area?		
Are areas under storage shelves kept clean regularly?		

Is food transported in a way that protects against contamination?		
Is the food area free of pests?		
Is there any sign of rodent or insect infestation?		
Does the dishwashing machine maintain 140° F for the wash cycle, and 180° F for the rinse cycle?		
For manual wash does the water temperature stay 170° F for 15 seconds?		
Does the 3 compartment sink use the sanitized solution per manufacturer recommendation?		
Is a log kept of the dishwashing machine wash and rinse temperature, as well as the 3 compartment sink sanitizing reading?		

F814–Dispose of Garbage and Refuse Properly

Is garbage and refuse container in good condition?		
Is waste properly contained in dumpsters or compactors with lids covered?		
Is the garbage storage area maintained in good condition to prevent harborage and feeding of pests?		
Are garbage receptacles covered when being removed from the kitchen area to the dumpster?		

NOTES

F880–Infection Control (Kitchen and Food Service)

Regulation & Interpretive Guidelines	Compliance Y / N / NA	Comments
Does the facility have a system to monitor and investigate causes of infection and manner of spread of infection?		
Does the facility program include risk assessment of occurrence of communicable disease for both residents and staff that is reviewed annually?		
Does the kitchen staff use gloves in accordance with kitchen standards		
Does facility prohibit staff with open areas on their skin, signs of infection or other indication of illness, from handling food products?		
Does staff know who to report potential communicable disease to internally?		
Does the kitchen have policy and procedures on infection prevention and control		

F908–Essential Equipment, Safe Operating Condition

Are the kitchen refrigerator and freezer in safe operating condition?		
Is the equipment maintained according to manufacturer recommendation?		
Is other kitchen equipment in safe operating condition?		

F925–Maintains Effective Pest Control Program

Does the facility demonstrate effective pest control program?		
Is the facility free from rodents and pests?		
Does facility have regular routine pest control treatments?		

NOTES

SURVEY & ENFORCEMENT PROCESS

FOR

SKILLED NURSING FACILITIES (SNFS)

AND

AND NURSING FACILITIES (NFS)

BRIEF SYNOPSIS

ENFORCEMENT PROCESS–BRIEF SYNOPSIS

Chapter 7 of the States Operations Manual also gives information about the Enforcement Process for Skilled Nursing Facilities (SNFs) and Nursing Facilities (NFs). After an annual certification survey, or any Federal or State survey, the long term care facilities, including skilled nursing facilities (SNFs) and nursing facilities (NFs) will be required to submit an acceptable plan of correction within the required timeframe, which is 10 calendar days from receipt of the deficiency report Form CMS-2567, if deficiencies are cited during the survey. If there are no deficiencies cited or if the deficiency is Level A, that means the facility has a very successful survey, that the facility is in substantial compliance and no plan of correction is required. If however a facility has an immediate jeopardy (IJ) citation for their survey, this clearly is an adverse outcome for the facility. A facility with an "IJ" will not be allowed to submit a plan of correction for their survey until *after* the facility removes the immediate jeopardy. Facilities must take immediate action to remove the IJ while the surveyors are still in the building during the survey, because an IJ means that there are situations going on in the facility that will cause adverse outcome, such as serious injury, harm, impairment, or death; or the likelihood that these adverse outcomes will occur. So administrator and his/her team must work very hard to remove the IJ.

ACCEPTABLE PLAN OF CORRECTION

ACCEPTABLE PLAN OF CORRECTION–ACCEPTABLE PLAN OF CORRECTION has been revised with an effective implementation date of November 16, 2018. Below is the revised acceptable plan of correction requirements: Implementation of 11/16/18:

Except in cases of past noncompliance, facilities having deficiencies (other than those at scope and severity level A) must submit an acceptable plan of correction. An acceptable plan of correction must:

- *Address how corrective action will be accomplished by the facility staff for those residents found to have been affected by the deficient practice;*

- *Address how the facility staff will identify other residents having the potential to be affected by the same deficient practice;*

- *Address what measures the facility staff will put into place or what systemic changes made to ensure that the deficient practice will not recur;*

- *Indicate how the facility staff plans to **monitor** its performance to make sure that solutions put in place are sustained; and*

- *Include dates when corrective action will be completed. The corrective action completion dates **must** be acceptable to the State. If the plan of correction is unacceptable for any reason, the State will notify the facility in writing. If the plan of correction is acceptable, the State will notify the facility by phone, email, etc. Facilities should be cautioned that they are ultimately accountable for their own compliance, and that responsibility is not alleviated in cases where notification about the acceptability of their plan of correction is not made timely.*

The **plan of correction** *serves as the facility's allegation of compliance with regulation and, without it; CMS and/or the State have no basis on which to verify compliance. A plan of correction must be submitted within 10 calendar days from the date the facility receives its Form CMS-2567, Deficiency Report. If an acceptable plan of correction is not received by the survey agency within this timeframe the State will notify the facility that it is recommending to the Regional Office (RO) of the Centers for Medicare and*

Medicaid Services and/or the State Medicaid Agency that remedies be imposed effective when notice requirements are not met.

It must be noted here that the law or regulation 42 CFR 488.45(b)(ii) require that CMS or the State to terminate the provider agreement of a facility that does not submit an acceptable plan of correction.

It must also be noted that a facility does not have to submit a plan of correction for a deficiency cited as past noncompliance because that deficiency is corrected at the time it is cited; however, the survey team must document the facility's corrective active actions on Form 2567.

REVISITS AND VERIFYING FACILITY COMPLIANCE

OF COURSE THE LONG TERM CARE PROFESSIONALS in the SNFs and NFs are very much familiar with the sequences of events after the survey and the steps facilities take to meet compliance. Revisits and the type of verifying of compliance depend on the deficiencies and scope and severity of those deficiencies that facilities receive.

The state operations manual states that while the plan of correction serves as the facility's allegations of compliance in non-immediate jeopardy cases, substantial compliance cannot be certified and any remedies imposed cannot be lifted until facility compliance has been verified.

- A mandatory onsite revisit is required when a facility's survey finds deficiencies that constitute substandard quality of care, harm, or immediate jeopardy. If the first revisit finds substantial compliance with the tags that were deficient, no continued onsite revisits are necessary for any other tags that are cited at or below level F.

- If the revisit still finds substandard quality of care, harm, or immediate jeopardy, there will be a second revisit.

- The facility will have to come in substantial compliance within the 6-month period, to avoid termination of its provider agreement. Two onsite revisits are permitted at the state's discretion without Regional Office approval. The Regional Office will have to give authorization in order for the State Agency to conduct more than two onsite revisits for SNFs only and/or dually participating facilities.

- **The purpose for the revisit** is for surveyors to verify facilities' substantial compliance.

- When a revisit is conducted for either a health survey or a life safety survey, but not both, there are separate revisit counts toward each survey.

- **An onsite visit to determine if immediate jeopardy** has been removed, that onsite visit will be included in the revisit count.

- **Timing of Revisit**—onsite revisits occur anytime from **the last correction date on the plan of correction and the 60th day from the survey date** to confirm that the facility is in substantial compliance.

- **Levels A, B, C, deficiencies**–are considered within the substantial compliance range, and may not be reviewed when surveyors conduct a revisit, if the facility had other deficiencies that fell outside the substantial compliance range.

- **Revisit for substandard quality of care, harm, and immediate jeopardy**–onsite revisit for these deficiencies will continue even if these lessen to lower levels of noncompliance.

ENFORCEMENT PROCESS

Listing of Enforcement Remedies for skilled Nursing Facilities (SNFs), Nursing Facilities (NFs), and Dually Participating Facilities (SNFs/NFs)–State Operations Manual §7400 (Revised 185, Issued: 11-16-18, Effective date of 11-16-18, and Implementation: 11-16-18).

Sections 1819(h) and 1919(h) of the Act, as well as 42 CFR §§488.404, 488.406 and 488.408, provide that CMS or the State may impose one or more remedies in addition to, or instead of, termination of the provider when the state or CMS finds that a facility is out of compliance with federal requirements. Enforcement protocols/procedures are based on the premise that all requirements must be met and take on greater or lesser significance depending on the specific circumstances and resident outcomes in each facility.

7400.1–Available Federal Enforcement remedies (Implemented 11-16-18)

In accordance with 42 CFR 488.406, the following remedies are available:

- Termination of the provider agreement;
- Temporary management;
- Denial of payment for all Medicare and/or Medicaid residents by CMS;
- Denial of payment for all new Medicare and/or Medicaid admissions;
- Civil Money penalties;
- State Monitoring;
- Transfer of residents;
- Transfer of residents with closure of facility;
- Directed plan of corrections;

- Directed in-service training; and

- Alternative or additional State remedies approved by CMS.

7400.2–Enforcement Remedies for the State Medicaid Agency (Implemented 11-16-18))

Regardless of what other remedies the State Medicaid Agency may want to establish in addition to the remedy of termination of the provider agreement, it must establish, at a minimum, the following statutorily-specified remedies or an approved alternative to these specified remedies:

- Temporary management;

- Denial of payment for all new admissions;

- Civil money penalties;

- Transfer of residents;

- Transfer of residents with closure of facility; and

- State monitoring.

THE DEFICIENCY MATRIX

Immediate Jeopardy to resident health or safety	J PoC Required Substandard quality of care	K PoC Required Substandard quality of care	L PoC Required Substandard quality of care
Actual harm that is not immediate	G PoC Required	H PPoC Required Substandard quality of care	I PoC Required Substandard quality of care
No actual harm with potential for more than minimal harm that is not immediate jeopardy	D PoC Required	E PoC Required	F PoC Required Substandard quality of care
No actual harm with potential for minimal harm	A No PoC Required No remedies Commitment to Correct Not on CMS-2567	B PoC Required	Level C PoC Required
	Isolated	Pattern	Widespread

Survey result/Deficiency report CMS Form-2567 with deficiencies of **A, B, & C only** means that the facility is in substantial compliance with the requirements of participation of the Medicare & Medicaid programs.

REFERENCES

State Operations Manual, Chapter 7–Survey and Enforcement Process for Skilled Nursing Facilities and Nursing Facilities (Rev.185, 1-16-18)

State Operations Manual, Appendix Q–Core Guidelines for Determining Immediate Jeopardy

State Operations Manual Appendix PP–Guidance to Surveyors for Long Term Care Facilities Effective November 28, 2017

CMS.gov–Long Term Care Survey Process (LLTCSP) Procedure Guide Effective May 5, 22019

Department of Health and Human Services Centers for Medicare & Medicaid Services Entrance Conference Worksheet 8/2017

Department of Health and Human Services Centers for Medicare & Medicaid Services Nutrition Critical Element Pathway

Department of Health and Human Services Centers for Medicare & Medicaid Services Kitchen Observation

CMS.gov–Centers for Medicare & Medicaid Services F-Tag Crosswalk

Medicare.gov website Nursing Home Compare

The Henry J. Kaiser Family Foundation May 2015, Reading the Stars: Nursing Home Quality Star Ratings, Nationally and by State. Boccuti, Casillas, Neumann

www.ingramcontent.com/pod-product-compliance
Lightning Source LLC
LaVergne TN
LVHW060202080526
838202LV00052B/4188